DESTINATION: LUXOR

A DANE MADDOCK ADVENTURE

DAVID WOOD
SEAN ELLIS

Destination: Luxor
Copyright 2018 by David Wood
All rights reserved

Published by Adrenaline Press
www.adrenaline.press

Adrenaline Press is an imprint of Gryphonwood
Press
www.gryphonwoodpress.com

Cover design by Bees' Knees Creatives

ISBN-13: 978-1-940095-85-1
ISBN-10: 1-940095-85-9

Dane Maddock and "Bones" Bonebrake journey up the Nile looking for treasure and adventure... And find trouble.

Dane and Bones have traveled to Luxor, Egypt, and the historic Valley of the Kings to explore a sunken subterranean passage that just might lead to the undiscovered tomb of a forgotten Pharaoh. But someone else has beaten them to it. A ruthless black-market art dealer wants the Pharaoh's riches for himself, and to hide his crimes, is prepared to unleash a deadly, ancient curse on an unsuspecting world.

DESTINATION: LUXOR is the second in a new series of stand-alone novellas by prolific action-adventure novelist Sean Ellis, featuring the characters from David Wood's bestselling Dane Maddock Adventures. Each new story in the DESTINATION: ADVENTURE series will transport Dane, Bones and the crew of Sea Foam to an exotic and exciting locale, where treasure, mystery, and adventure await!

Praise for David Wood and Sean Ellis!

"Dane and Bones.... Together they're unstoppable. Rip roaring action from start to finish. Wit and humor throughout. Just one question - how soon until the next one? Because I can't wait." -*Graham Brown, author of Shadows of the Midnight Sun*

"What an adventure! A great read that provides lots of action, and thoughtful insight as well, into strange realms that are sometimes best left unexplored." -*Paul Kemprecos, author of Cool Blue Tomb and the NUMA Files*

BOOKS and SERIES by DAVID WOOD

The Dane Maddock Adventures
Dourado
Cibola
Quest
Icefall
Buccaneer
Atlantis
Ark
Xibalba
Loch
Solomon Key

Dane and Bones Origins
Freedom
Hell Ship
Splashdown
Dead Ice
Liberty
Electra
Amber
Justice
Treasure of the Dead

Adventures from the Dane Maddock Universe
Destination-Rio
Destination-Luxor
Berserk
The Tomb
Devil's Face
Outpost

Arcanum
Magus
Brainwash
Herald
Maug

Jade Ihara Adventures (with Sean Ellis)
Oracle
Changeling
<u>Exile</u>

Bones Bonebrake Adventures
Primitive
The Book of Bones
Skin and Bones
Venom

Jake Crowley Adventures (with Alan Baxter)
Blood Codex
<u>Anubis Key</u>

Brock Stone Adventures
Arena of Souls
Track of the Beast (forthcoming)

Myrmidon Files (with Sean Ellis)
Destiny
<u>Mystic</u>

Sam Aston Investigations (with Alan Baxter)
<u>Primordial</u>
<u>Overlord</u>

Stand-Alone Novels
Into the Woods (with David S. Wood)
Callsign: Queen (with Jeremy Robinson)
Dark Rite (with Alan Baxter)

David Wood writing as David Debord

The Absent Gods Trilogy
The Silver Serpent
Keeper of the Mists
The Gates of Iron

The Impostor Prince (with Ryan A. Span)
Neptune's Key
The Zombie-Driven Life
You Suck

BOOKS and SERIES by SEAN ELLIS

The Nick Kismet Adventures
The Shroud of Heaven
Into the Black
The Devil You Know (Novella)
Fortune Favors

The Adventures of Dodge Dalton
In the Shadow of Falcon's Wings
At the Outpost of Fate
On the High Road to Oblivion
Against the Fall of Eternal Night (with Kerry Frey)

FROM THE AUTHORS

This story includes the names of several historical figures. These names are used fictitiously. We have also changed the names of certain historical characters who might be familiar to you. Hope you enjoy the story!

PROLOGUE

Captain Roger Bell, personal secretary to Howard Carter, mopped his brow and took a deep breath of the parched air. It was a hot, sunny day in the Valley of the Kings, with highs approaching 25 Celsius of late. He was tired: tired of the heat, tired of the dust, and tired of Carter's obsession. Of course, Bell had known early on what sort of man Carter was, and knew that same obsession just might drive him to greatness. And today, they perhaps stood on the precipice of a magnificent discovery.

Experts agreed that the Valley of the Kings had long ago given up all its secrets. Countless archaeologists had scoured the valley, digging up everything they could find that thousands of years of tomb robbers hadn't manage to carry away. It was only the legend of ancient curses that served to deter some of the latter. Some, but not all. Nevertheless, Carter had insisted that there were still wonders waiting to be unearthed in this place. Undeterred, Carter kept searching.

"What do you reckon?" a voice asked.

Bell recognized the odd accent immediately.

Arthur Cruttenden Mace, known to most as A.C., was a Tasmanian-born Egyptologist and a member of the excavation team. He was a lean man with overlarge ears, dark hair, and thick mustache. His skin was tan and weathered from working in the unforgiving Egyptian climate, but his eyes shone with youthful vigor.

"I don't dare hope," Bell admitted. "He's been disappointed too many times before."

Carter had begun work in 1914, only to be interrupted by the Great War. Work resumed in 1917 as Carter continued on what many considered a fool's errand: the search for the tomb of a little-known pharaoh named Tutankhamun. He cited several pieces of evidence a faience cup, a piece of gold foil, and a cache of funerary items, all bearing the name of Tutankhamun, as proof that the pharaoh had, in fact, lived, died, and was buried somewhere in the valley. He further vowed to dig "down to the bedrock" if need be. Not everyone was persuaded, but all agreed on one thing: the tomb of Tutankhamun, if it existed, had not yet been found. Five years later, hope waned in everyone except Carter.

"Don't be like that," Mace chided. "Wasn't it you who predicted the staircase would just lead back to Rameses' tomb?"

Bell nodded. Three weeks earlier, in what Carter grudgingly vowed would be his final season of excavation here, the team had uncovered a step carved into the bedrock near the tomb of Rameses VI. Though Bell had been skeptical, Carter insisted it was the breakthrough they'd been searching for.

Days of digging and clearing rubble revealed a staircase, which had led to a sealed door. The plastered door bore no names, but they identified seals of the royal necropolis. Hope sparked anew, though Bell still tempered his with a healthy dose of skepticism. Fearing grave robbers, Carter and his team had covered the steps over again, leaving them that way until they received word of the arrival of their chief financier, Lord

Carnarvon and his daughter, Lady Evelyn Herbert, in Luxor three days ago.

"Well, he was right about it being Tutankhamun," Bell said. "I just hope there's still something there to be found." When the crew had uncovered the steps again, along with the door, in anticipation of Lord Carnarvon's arrival, they had found Tutankhamen's name at the bottom. Their joy had been somewhat tempered by the realization that the door was not fully sealed. Someone had broken through the corner and sealed it again. They were not the first to discover the tomb. Behind that door, they had found and cleared a twenty-six foot passage, which ended at another, door, one that had also been resealed in antiquity.

"I think we're going to find riches," Mace said. "Just because the door was-re-sealed, it doesn't necessarily mean that robbers have completely looted it, or taken anything from it at all. Certainly nothing larger than the small hole they opened. And the fact that no artifacts associated with Tutankhamun have surface, that gives me hope."

"Let's just hope it hasn't been cursed," Bell joked.

Mace ignored him. "I don't see any newspaper men. Hopefully we've finally confounded them."

Word of a potential discovery had somehow reached local journalists. Fearing Carter would attempt to open the tomb without government officials present, they'd circled like carrion birds for days. Meanwhile, Carter had quietly coordinated for the tomb to be opened on a Friday afternoon, when the tourists were gone and all the important players would be present. Hopefully they would be able to do this undisturbed.

"There's Carnarvon now." Mace said. "I suppose it's

time."

His mouth suddenly dryer than the desert that surrounded him, Bell nodded and followed Mace. A small group had gathered, and he recognized several faces, though he didn't know all the names.

Carter took the lead, followed by Mace and Arthur Callender, known to friends as "Pecky." The three led the way down to the sealed door. A barrier had been constructed before it, and the men moved around behind it. Carter, stripped down to his vest and trousers, paused to make a speech, which Bell barely heard over the pounding of his heart. The moment had almost arrived! Leave it to Carter to stretch things out after so many years of searching. The man was clearly driving home the point that he had been right, and all the so-called experts wrong, about Tutankhamen.

At long last, it was time to open the tomb. While the onlookers kept their distance, Carter was ready to begin. They watched as he located the wooden lintel above the door and began removing the small stone beneath it. When he had broken through, he pushed a long rod into the hole.

"Open space behind," he announced.

Excited whispers broke out among the onlookers. They waited impatiently as the men conducted candle tests to check for the presence of poison gases. Finally satisfied it was safe, Carter thrust a candle through the opening and peered inside.

Silence hung over those assembled as Carter stood frozen in place. The man did not move.

What did he mean by it? Bell wondered. Was the tomb empty. Had some strange gas paralyzed him? Was there, in fact, a curse?

Unable to stand the suspense, Lord Carnarvon blurted, "Can you see anything?"

Another pause, and then Carter spoke softly.

"Yes. Wonderful things."

February 20, 1930
St. James, London, England

Roger Lane Powell Bell, third Baron Grayson, poured himself a glass of sherry and strode to the window of his seventh floor St. James apartment. He gazed out at the night sky that cloaked London in a darkness that paled beside that which filled his heart.

In his right hand he clutched the letter from Howard Carter. It was not the sole cause of his black mood, but it had deepened his despair and fueled his anger.

He glanced down at it again, his eyes scarcely taking in the text.

"...*this talk of a curse is utter nonsense...*"

"The hell with you, Carter," he muttered.

He sank down in the chair closest to the window and took a sip of sherry, savoring the way it burned its way down his throat. It was like fire, but it could not cleanse him. Perhaps nothing could.

"No curse." He barked a sharp laugh. He knew there was a curse. Its hand upon the world was evident. It was even inside of him!

He crumpled Carter's letter into a ball and flung it in the direction of the fireplace. He missed badly, but didn't care.

"How can the man be so blind?" he whispered. He had written to Carter, laying out the evidence that proved the curse of the Pharaohs was real. He wasn't certain what he was hoping for. Perhaps some arcane knowledge Carter had uncovered in Egypt that could counter the curse. There had to be a cure. He'd tried doctors and priests, but nothing could cure what burned inside him.

He stood and began pacing. The names rang inside his head. He had long ago learned them by heart.

Lord Carnarvon, died four months after the opening of the tomb.

George Jay Gould I, died one month later.

Prince Ali Kamel Fahmy Bey of Egypt and Colonel Aubrey Herbert both died later that same year.

The list went on.

Sir Archibald Douglas-Reid, the radiologist who x-rayed Tutankhamun's mummy, died just over a year later from a mysterious illness.

Sir Lee Stack, Governor-General of Sudan.

A.C. Mace, a key member of Carter's excavation team.

Mervyn Herbert, Lord Carnarvon's half-brother.

And his own son, Captain Roger Bell, secretary to Howard Carter.

All had entered the tomb of Tutankhamen.

And all were dead.

A wave of grief washed over him, and he stood and rushed to the locked cabinet on the other side of the room. He opened it with trembling hands and stared at the contents.

A collection of artifacts stared back at him: a scarab, a lamp, a dagger, a chalice, even a vial that had once contained perfume. All were items his son had taken from the tomb and given to his father. He knew he ought to feel repulsed by the sight of them, but they were a tangible link to the child he had lost.

On an impulse he picked up the vial of perfume, uncapped it, and held it to his nose. He inhaled deeply, imagining he could breathe in the scents of ancient Egypt, imagined he was reunited with his son. He could almost see the two of them strolling in the shadows of the great pyramids. This had become a regular ritual since his son's death, a veritable compulsion. Several times a day he handled the artifacts, running his hands over the scarab, and along the blade of the dagger. Breathing in the long-vanished scent of perfume. Even sipping water from the chalice.

He breathed in again and his sinuses burned. A series of ragged coughs tore through his chest, the ensuing dizziness brought him to his knees.

Ghostly images swam before his eyes. Ghosts and demons.

He wasn't getting better. He would not recover, of this he was certain.

All he wanted was to be free of this curse and reunited with his son.

His eyes fell on the open window and he made up his mind.

ONE

"**Are you sure** we're in the right country?"

Dane Maddock glanced over at his friend and partner, Uriah "Bones" Bonebrake, sighed, and braced himself for another awful joke. "Why do you ask?"

"We've been here two days and I haven't seen anyone walking like this." Without breaking stride, Bones turned and struck an odd pose—wrists, elbows and knees bent at sharp angles, his left hand bobbing sinuously in front of his face like a cobra about to strike, his right held at the small of his back like a duck's tail. The effect was somewhat blunted by the large beige and black Pelican BA-22 carry-on case he gripped in his right hand, and the even larger hockey gear bag slung over one shoulder, but that didn't stop him from adopting a falsetto voice and vocalizing what Maddock assumed was meant to be the harmony from a Bangles' song. "Way-oh-way-ohhh-way-ohohohh. Walk like an Egyptian."

His antics earned a few curious glances from passersby, but the faces just as quickly looked away, clearly intimidated by his appearance. At six feet-five inches, Bones towered above everyone, including the almost six-foot-tall Maddock, but the height disparity was only part of it. Bones' Native American heritage gave him a dark complexion, not unlike the skin-tone of the Egyptians around them, but his long pony tail and complete lack of facial hair distinctly set him apart as something else entirely.

Maddock regarded his friend for a few seconds and then, in his best approximation of a Jeopardy contestant, said, "Who is Steve Martin?"

Bones frowned. "Steve Martin?" He shook his head. "Dude, I worry about you sometimes."

"If you don't know who Steve Martin is, maybe I should be worried about you."

"I know who Steve Martin is," Bones shot back, sourly. "I just don't see what he has to do with this."

"You're kidding, right? King Tut?" Maddock, fully aware that it was completely out of character for him, nevertheless adopted a pose similar to what Bones had displayed, and sing-songed, "'How'd you get so funk-y? Did you do the mon-key?'"

Bones just blinked at him.

"Born in Arizona, moved to Babylonia?"

Bones shook his head. "Susannah Hoffs versus Steve Martin, and you go with the old white dude? I guess I shouldn't be surprised."

Maddock resumed walking down the train platform, passing ornate columns—replicas of the actual historic artifacts that were ubiquitous throughout the region—interspersed with vending machines. "I would have thought you, of all people, would like that song."

Bones snorted. "Keep singing. Even if I don't figure it out, at least it will scare the locals off."

As if on cue, a young Egyptian man, bolder than the others, stepped in front of them. "Taxi? You need taxi?"

Despite his impulse to politely dismiss the man, Maddock simply ignored him. Showing even a little deference would only encourage more offers, or so all the guidebooks said, and since most of the supplicants were actually con artists hoping to bilk unwary tourists with bait-and-switch games, there was no reason to feel bad about being a little rude.

The Egyptian repeated the offer a couple more times, then fell back, setting his sights on someone else disembarking from the overnight express train, but another entrepreneur quickly took his place. Unlike the first Egyptian, who had been wearing Western attire, this man wore a more traditional *jellabiya* long garment of light blue cotton, and a white turban.

"Camel ride? You want camel ride? Just seventy-five pounds. Valley of the Kings? Deir el-Bahari? My cousin take you there."

They actually were headed for the first location, the famed archaeological site, where in 1922, archaeologist Howard Carter had discovered the treasure-laden tomb of Pharaoh Tutankhamun, but despite the fact that seventy-five Egyptian pounds converted to about five American dollars, Maddock was wary of both the offer and the suggested mode of transportation.

Bones either shared his antipathy or couldn't resist the opening for an off-color joke. "I'm not getting my moose knuckle anywhere near a camel toe."

Maddock groaned and dead-panned. "Didn't see that coming."

"You know," Bones went on, conversationally, as they continued down the platform, leaving the camel-tour vendor behind, "when you said we had a job in Luxor, this wasn't exactly what came to mind."

Maddock had heard variations on this theme several times during the flight to Cairo and the subsequent overnight train ride along the Nile River. Bones had been crestfallen to learn that they were headed to Egypt instead of to the Luxor Casino on the Las Vegas Strip, although he had commented that he was not a fan of the Luxor's elevator, which ascended and descended at a forty-five degree angle.

"We're treasure hunters, Bones. People don't find treasure in Vegas. They lose it. I'm saving you from a lot of heartache and disappointment. Besides. I would have thought you'd be sick of casinos by now." Bones' uncle, Crazy Charlie, operated a casino on the Cherokee reservation in North Carolina. Bones had even briefly worked there as a bouncer after leaving the military.

"It's not about the gambling, dude. It's the chicks!" Bones looked around and wrinkled his nose distastefully. "Next time you get the urge to save me from anything... don't. And if you think there's any treasure left to be found here, you're fooling yourself. This place was picked clean thousands of years ago. Now it's just another tourist trap in the desert, only with more flies and dysentery."

"You seem to have forgotten what we discovered the last time we were here."

"We almost got killed and we didn't find any treasure."

Although it was hard to argue with any of what Bones had just said, Maddock knew that there were still serious archaeological discoveries being made in the desert surrounding Luxor. There was far too much history in Egypt for everything of value to have been uncovered. It was just such a discovery that had brought the two of them here.

Maddock might have called them "treasure hunters" but he was motivated more by his passion for history and exploration, not to mention a craving for adventure, than by mere lust for gold. While he needed to make a living like anyone, it was the looking not the finding that satisfied the yearning in his soul. He also knew that

Bones, despite his rough edges, felt the same way, which was why their partnership had flourished, despite getting off to a rocky start.

They had met in the Navy, during the first phase of SEAL training. Maddock, had been an uptight young officer looking to advance his career, and Bones had been a hard-drinking, hard-partying enlisted seaman with a chip on his shoulder as big as the Cherokee Nation. Against all odds, the two men had become friends, and then after leaving the service, had gone into business together as marine salvage and recovery experts. In the years that had followed, the two men had made astonishing discoveries in every far-flung corner of the globe, and saved the world once or twice along the way. Recently, they had started doing contract work for the Global Heritage Commission, a small agency working under the auspices of the United Nations, dedicated to protecting World Heritage sites. Most of their jobs involved underwater surveys, helping marine archaeologists document wrecks and submerged ruins. There was very little treasure involved, and even less glory, but it was satisfying work and it kept the lights on. Even more important to Maddock, it was an excuse to spend time underwater.

This particular job, which had brought them to the Egyptian desert, would probably not afford him a chance to get wet. An Egyptian archaeologist named Dr. Majdy, working in the Valley of the Kings on the west bank of the Nile River, had discovered an unfinished royal tomb containing what had initially appeared to be a deep cistern, still partially filled with water. Subsequent tests however indicated that the water in the cistern was fresh, and chemically identical to that found in the Nile River, nearly three miles away. Since it was not being replenished by rainwater, or any other external source, the only logical assumption was that it was not a cistern, but rather a well, probably fed by an uncharted subterranean tributary of the Nile. A dye test would likely confirm the existence of a passage connecting the well to the river, but Majdy wanted to conduct a survey to see if it might be part of an ancient water supply system, connecting to other undiscovered chambers, and to that end had contacted the Global Heritage Commission for technical assistance in conducting an underwater survey, which was how Maddock and Bones had gotten involved.

The actual survey would be done using a small ROV—remotely-operated-vehicle—which Bones carried in the Pelican case. Not quite a meter long, and no bigger around than a gallon milk jug, the ROV—nicknamed Uma—could go places a person couldn't, which was advantageous since the water level in the cistern was more than a hundred feet down, and there was no telling what lay below the surface. Even if subterranean passages did lead back to the river, it was extremely unlikely that the channels would be large enough to accommodate a diver, but just in case, they had also brought along SCUBA gear.

They were hit up several more times as they made their way off the platform to pass through the station. There were offers of taxi service, camel safaris, and hot air balloon tours. One young man slyly inquired if they were interested in purchasing "authentic" ancient Egyptian artifacts. Maddock had to maintain a fierce grip on the strap of his gear bag to prevent some of the men from simply grabbing it off his shoulder. He didn't know if their intent was merely to bear his luggage to his taxi or hotel and then extort a large gratuity from him, or to simply abscond with it. It seemed prudent to leave that particular mystery unsolved.

The train station was decorated to resemble an ancient Egyptian temple, with white alabaster columns and false balconies inside, and an exterior sandstone beige façade adorned with an enormous stylized Egyptian vulture with outstretched golden wings above the entrance. A short flight of steps led down to the pavement where a line of taxis were waiting to bear the arriving passengers to their next destination. Maddock paused on the steps, letting the herd thin out a bit as he got his first good look at the city of Luxor.

First occupied more than five thousand years before the present, the city had been known to the ancient Egyptians as Wo'se—City of the Sceptre, signifying its status as the administrative center of Upper Egypt—and later as Niwt-'Imn—City of Amun, the chief deity of southern Egypt. Situated on the banks of the Nile River, about four hundred miles upriver from Cairo—or Memphis, as it was known in ancient times—the city had for a time, served as the capital of the unified Egyptian Kingdom. Many of the best-known names in ancient Egyptian history had lived, died and been buried there. The Greeks called it Thebes of the Hundred Gates, but by the time of Alexander the Great, the city's importance had already begun to wane, and by the First Century, it had become little more than a memory. The rediscovery of the ancient ruins by Napoleon's savants—scientific scholars who accompanied his invasion force in 1798— had not only resulted in the creation of the new science of Egyptology, but had also brought renewed interest in the Arab settlement known as al-ʾUqṣur—the Palaces—later simplified to Luxor. Cairo had the pyramids and the Sphinx, but the real treasures of ancient Egypt were hidden in the sands outside Luxor, and despite more than two centuries of archaeological exploration—and five millennia of looting by tomb robbers, not all of them had been uncovered.

Modern Luxor looked to Maddock like an eclectic hodge-podge of weathered old Colonial-era architecture and newer utilitarian structures of brick and concrete. To his left, he could see the minaret of a mosque reaching up like an exclamation point from behind another building, while a few hundred yards in the opposite direction rose the white dome and bell towers of a Coptic Orthodox Church. The one-way two-lane street fronting the railway station was shared by cars and buses, as well as old motorcycles, donkey carts and even ornate horse-drawn four-wheeled carriages—called *caleches*. The air was hot and dry, despite the close proximity of the river, but while there were no clouds in the azure sky, there were strange bulbous shapes visible in the west, just above the horizon—hot air balloons, drifting on the wind.

He was still gazing up at them when he heard Bones calling to him. "Dude, I think that's our ride."

Maddock returned his attention to the pick-up lane and saw that an older-model red Peugeot sedan had slipped into the queue of blue-and-white liveried cabs. The passenger side window had been lowered and the driver was leaning across to wave a hand at them. They had been told to expect a car, but there was no way of knowing if this was actually it, or just one more local entrepreneur looking to score some tourist cash.

"I hope you're right," Maddock replied, starting forward.

As he drew closer, he was surprised to see that the driver was a woman. She appeared to be young—late twenties, perhaps—with olive complexion and fine features, but that was about all he could tell about her. The rest of her head was covered by a black *hijab* scarf.

A woman?

The revelation stopped him in his tracks.

He had seen quite a few women since arriving in Egypt the previous day, but had not actually interacted with any of them. Everybody he had dealt with—from the customs officials at the airport to the endless stream of touts at the station—had been male. The distribution of the sexes among his fellow travelers—both Egyptian and non-Egyptian—had been pretty even, so the disparity hadn't really registered with him

Although predominately Muslim, Egypt was not as strict about enforcing gender segregation as some neighboring countries, at least where visitors were concerned, but it was a different story for the locals, particularly in Upper Egypt, far from the more relaxed atmosphere of metropolitan centers like Cairo and Alexandria. Despite some progressive reforms during the Twentieth Century, the more recent rise in religious fundamentalism coupled with a flagging economy, had severely limited opportunities for women in a country that had once been ruled by the likes of Nefertiti and Cleopatra. The situation for Egyptian women was, by some accounts, the worst in the Arab world, with the highest rates of sexual harassment, honor killings and female genital mutilation.

Maddock knew from experience that interacting

with a local female under such conditions might very well make her the subject of such abuse. *Maybe a case of mistaken identity?*

The woman locked eyes with him. Hers were almond-shaped and a deep chocolate brown. Then she smiled. No lipstick, but her teeth were dazzling. "Mr. Maddox?"

So much for that idea. "Uh… It's Maddock, actually," he said, stressing the last syllable.

She blinked, her sculpted eyebrows coming together in a look of confusion. "What's the difference?"

Maddock glanced around, checking to see if the exchange had attracted any undue attention, and discovered that at least one person had taken an interest.

"Here's how I remember it," Bones said, leaning down to get a better look at her. "Daffy is one mad duck. Singular. Donald and Daffy together would be mad ducks. Plural." He jerked a thumb in Maddock's direction. "He's just daffy."

Bones had clearly put a lot of thought into this explanation.

The woman blinked again, but her smile broadened, revealing dimples in her cheeks. "So just 'mad duck,'" she said. Her English was impeccable, with just a hint of a British accent. "I'll try to remember that."

"I wouldn't worry too much about it," Bones went on. "He's so desperate, he'll answer to anything. I'm Bones, but you can call me anytime."

"You are a very strange man, Anytime."

Maddock felt a mild surge of panic at his friend's typically forward behavior. What might get him a slap or a drink thrown in his face anywhere else could get him— or the woman—in serious trouble here. He stepped forward, intent on putting himself between Bones and the woman, but a flash of movement from the rear end of the car distracted him. As he turned to look, he saw a group of Egyptian men—a dozen, maybe more—closing with them, the nearest just a few steps away. All wore *jellabiyas* with turbans wrapped around heads and necks, but unlike the touts and scam artists who had been assailing them from the moment they stepped off the train, these men were strangely silent.

Maddock felt a tingle of apprehension. "Bones, I think—"

Before he could complete the thought, one of the men shouted something, and then, as if possessed of a single consciousness, they all charged.

TWO

The men crashed into them like linebackers converging on the quarterback, bowling both Maddock and Bones over. What the men individually lacked in size and weight, they more than made up for with strength of numbers. Maddock instinctively rounded his shoulders tucking into a protective ball as he fell back to land on his backside. The impact would probably leave bruises, but the rush of adrenaline through his bloodstream masked any pain. He felt tension on the strap of his bag as someone tried to wrench it free, and immediately tightened his grip on it, then rolled over onto it. It was a common tactic for purse snatchers to carry razor blades with which to cut purse straps as a way of quickly overcoming resistance. By covering the bag with his body, he was pre-empting such a measure; he just hoped the thieves didn't slash his exposed back instead.

If the bag had merely contained clothing, he probably wouldn't have risked it, but since it held a couple thousand dollars' worth of diving equipment, which could not be replaced on short notice and without which the entire trip to Egypt would be a complete waste of time and money, he decided to put up a bit more of a fight than was perhaps prudent. The men had not been displaying weapons, and he felt certain their plan had been to hit-and-run. If he was wrong….

He wasn't. His assailant immediately let go, and when Maddock looked up, he saw the Egyptians already fleeing the scene, the last of them cutting around the front end of the parked Peugeot and heading for the street beyond.

Maddock rolled off the bag, pushing up on hands

and knees. He found his friend, a few feet away, likewise in the process of recovering from the blindside attack. "Bones, you okay?"

"No, damn it," came the growled reply. "They got Uma!"

Even as he said it, Maddock realized that the Pelican case Bones had carried halfway around the world was now conspicuously absent. He bounded up and threw himself onto the hood of the Peugeot, sliding across it to land on his feet, ready to charge after the fleeing thieves.

He caught a glimpse of the man lugging the Pelican case, just as the latter ducked between two of the dozen or so horse drawn caleche carriages standing idle between the taxi queue and the main thoroughfare. Maddock sprinted for the same gap, but before he could reach it, the entire line of carriages began moving, peeling away to enter the flow of traffic.

He veered to the right, running faster in a futile attempt to get in front of the horse that now blocked his path. The animal was moving at a trot, not fast, but fast enough to keep Maddock from getting past. After a few seconds, he gave up, skidding to a stop and reversing direction, trying instead to cut behind the carriage.

Bones had regained his feet and was likewise looking for an opening to get through the jumble. "Do you see him?" he shouted.

Maddock didn't waste his breath answering in the negative. He had to get around the carriage, had to get a visual fix on the thief. If he couldn't, the odds of them ever seeing the little submersible drone again were virtually nil, and unlike the SCUBA equipment, replacing the ROV wasn't as simple as just submitting an insurance claim or writing a check. Uma was one-of-a-kind, built from scratch and custom programmed for a very specific range of operations. Without it, he and Bones wouldn't just be stymied for the duration of this job—they would be sidelined for weeks, maybe even months. He slapped a hand against the rear of the carriage, pushing it—or pushing himself away from it—as he ran around behind it, only to nearly crash into another.

Suddenly, the carriages were everywhere he wanted to go, weaving back and forth randomly... No, there was nothing random about it. The caleche drivers were intentionally running interference for the thieves. A glance up into the sneering face of the closest driver was enough to confirm this suspicion.

Maddock gave up trying to get through the tangle, and instead pulled himself up onto the running board of the carriage now blocking his path. From this elevated perch, he had a mostly unobstructed view of the street, but saw no sign of the stolen Pelican case, nor any of the men who had blitzed them.

Where did they go?

Movement in the corner of his eye arrested his attention, and he turned to see the carriage driver swinging a long-handled horse whip at his face. Maddock easily blocked the clumsy attack, swatting the whip away with one hand, and reaching out to grab the front of the man's robes with the other, but as he did, he realized that there was a passenger in the coach seat, someone he recognized. He had actually seen the man twice before; first on the platform, offering camel rides, and then again as part of the gang that had waylaid them.

Realization dawned. The drivers weren't merely running interference for the thieves; they were providing getaway transportation. He yanked the driver off his feet, pulling him over the back of the coachman's seat, and hurled him into his accomplice. The two men offered no further resistance, but merely covered their heads and started wailing, as if Maddock was the criminal and they were the aggrieved party. Maddock turned away, searching the nearby caleches for the missing bag, but most of the carriages had already pulled away and were now trundling down the street, their occupants eclipsed from view by raised sun canopies.

"Bones. Check the carriages!" Maddock shouted, and then, without looking back to see if the other man had heard him, dropped down to the pavement and charged after the retreating caleches. He first heard and then glimpsed Bones sprinting to catch up to him.

Ahead, the carriages had regrouped into a single line occupying the right lane, while cars and motorcycles whizzed by in the left. The coach drivers maintained tight spacing, allowing no gaps through which Maddock and Bones might reach the relative safety of the sidewalk, which left the men with a choice: risk injury or death by running down the middle of the traffic lanes, or abandon the pursuit.

Maddock knew the latter choice wasn't really an option; they couldn't lose Uma. Before he could commit however, a cacophony of honking horns erupted behind him. He shot a quick glance over his shoulder, expecting to see a taxi bearing down on him, and was instead pleasantly surprised to see the red Peugeot, moving slowly up the inside lane behind them. The increasingly irate honking was coming from the long stream of vehicles behind it.

"She's blocking for us," Bones shouted.

Maddock just nodded. Bolstered by the unexpected assistance, he poured on a burst of speed to catch the next caleche in line. As he got alongside it, he reached out a hand to seize the black canopy, ripping it back to expose the interior of the passenger area.

The carriage was empty.

He let go, dodging a wild swing from the driver's whip as it whistled above his head, and veered back into the street. Bones had pulled ahead of him and was now just a few steps away from catching the next carriage in line. Maddock looked past his friend, counting the remaining caleches. There were six in all, the one in the lead now a good fifty yards ahead. Reasoning that the thief would probably have gone to the head of the line, he abandoned his original plan to check each carriage in turn, and instead pounded up the street, giving the carriages a wide berth.

Maddock was in better than average physical shape, but the hot climate and the additional burden of the SCUBA equipment in his bag were taking a toll. Perspiration streamed from his forehead, stinging his eyes. Despite his best efforts to regulate his breathing, his lungs burned with the need for more oxygen. He halved the distance to the lead carriage in less than ten seconds, passing three of the horse drawn vehicles, but with each successive step, his fatigue increased. A dark corona was blurring the periphery of his vision, a sure sign that heat exhaustion was creeping up on him.

Suddenly, the lead carriage veered left, cutting across his path even though it was a good fifteen yards ahead of him. The second carriage followed, forcing him to slow to avoid a collision. It took a moment for him to grasp that this wasn't some new defensive tactic but rather a change forced by the street itself, which as near as he could tell turned sharply to the left, running alongside the Coptic church he had earlier glimpsed. Maddock adjusted course, angling to intercept the lead carriage. The driver turned toward him, whip in hand, but this time Maddock was ready. As he got within striking distance, he unslung his bag and hefted it onto his left shoulder, using it as a shield. The whip struck the bag with a single impotent *thwock* as Maddock scrambled up onto the footboard and then broadsided the driver, slamming the bag into him and blasting him off the elevated platform and onto the sidewalk below.

Maddock's satisfaction was short-lived however. As he whirled to face the covered coach seat, he saw that, while there was a passenger—undoubtedly one of the escaping thieves—the case containing Uma was not there. Undeterred, Maddock leapt over the driver's seat, ramming his knee into the passenger's gut before the man could even think about fighting back. He then shoved the shade canopy down, clearing the obstruction to get a look at the second carriage.

The Pelican case was not there, either.

Further back, Bones was systematically working his way up from the rear, checking the caleches Maddock had bypassed, but to no better effect. He met Maddock's stare and shook his head angrily. "Where the hell is it?"

Maddock had no answer but he wasn't ready to give up. Maybe the carriages had been a bluff, a diversion to send the two of them on a wild goose chase. The Pelican case was awkward and heavy enough to make escape on foot an iffy proposition. If the thief was running, he couldn't have gotten far. Maddock swept his gaze back down the street toward the train station. He didn't see the thief, but he did see the red Peugeot, and its driver. She was leaning out the window, looking up at him inquisitively and shouting something. He couldn't hear her over the tumult of honking horns, but he could make a rough guess. *Did you catch him? Did you find it?*

Her question answered his own. She hadn't seen the thief, which meant he had not made his escape anywhere within her line of sight.

Maddock swung his gaze back to the line of now-motionless caleches, looking to the other side, which had mostly been hidden from his view during the pursuit. Once past the train station, the road ran parallel to the train tracks up to the point where it turned away at a ninety-degree angle. The tracks kept going, past the church heading north, but Maddock now saw that the turn wasn't a turn at all, but a T-junction. To the left, the wide avenue meandered west, bearing most of the traffic that had slipped past the Peugeot, but the street also continued in the other direction, past a marked railroad crossing, to disappear into the urban landscape.

A single carriage was heading down that street.

"There he is!" Maddock shouted, stabbing a finger toward the retreating vehicle before scrambling down from his perch to take up the pursuit once again. If he was wrong and Uma wasn't in the carriage, then all would be lost, but his instincts told him otherwise. He bounded across the railroad tracks and ran flat out. Bones appeared beside him, having evidently forced his way between two of the carriages, and pulled away. His long legs gave him a slight advantage in a running race, but Maddock suspected it was the other man's anger at losing Uma that fueled his furious sprint. Ahead, the carriage made a right turn, swinging down a side street.

Bones reached the same corner a few seconds later, and Maddock was right behind him.

Maddock immediately felt an oppressive sense of claustrophobia. The street was narrow, barely a single lane wide, and the buildings to either side rose up like sheer walls, three stories high, with balconies extending out overhead. Worse, he couldn't see past the carriage to the far end, if there even was one.

Was this a trap?

Before he could give voice to this new concern, Bones caught hold of the back end of the carriage and then, after another step or two brought himself—and the horse-drawn vehicle—to a dead stop. The caleche jolted and the sound of hooves skittering on dusty cobblestones filled the air, but Bones didn't budge.

Maddock reached him a moment later, sidling into the gap between the carriage and the brick wall on the left. As he passed, he pulled down the canopy to expose the interior. The passenger seat was empty, but removing the shade cover gave him an unobstructed view of the street ahead. The driver was still shaking the reins, trying to motivate the horse to overcome the resistance from Bones' "brakes," but just beyond the animal, a lone Egyptian in a powder blue *jellabiyah* and white turban was continuing on foot. He was trying to run, but his efforts were hampered by the burden he was carrying in his right hand.

The mere sight of the missing case invigorated Maddock like a shot of pure oxygen. He wriggled past the carriage and then sprinted the remaining few yards to tackle the thief with one outflung arm. As the man went sprawling, face first, he lost his grip on the stolen Pelican case which skidded noisily along the cobble pavement for another ten feet. Maddock kept going, reaching down to snag the case's handle, but as he rose back to his full height, he realized why the carriage had turned down the narrow alley in the first place. Thirty feet ahead to his right, the wall opened into what he guessed was a garage entrance. The interior space beyond was hidden in shadow, but in the instant that Maddock glimpsed it, four men stepped out into the light.

They looked Egyptian, but unlike the thieves and carriage drivers, they wore western attire—chinos and untucked long-sleeved dress shirts. They were also a good deal more physically imposing than the thieves and most of the other locals Maddock had seen, and judging by the hard stares they were giving him, were accustomed to using their size to intimidate others. Maddock didn't know if there was such a thing as the Egyptian Mafia, but if there was, these men were definitely enforcers. Whoever or whatever they were, it was plainly evident that the thief had been hoping to find refuge with them. Even now, prone on the pavement, he was jabbering at them. In unison, fists balled in preparation to do violence. the four men advanced toward Maddock.

Maddock knew that if he struck first, and struck hard, he might be able to sideline two of the men— provided they weren't as tough as they appeared—but that would still leave him at a numerical disadvantage. He would have liked his odds a lot better with Bones to back him up, but his partner was still on the other side of the stalled carriage. Breaking contact—the military euphemism for turning tail and running like hell—was clearly the better choice, but with the added burden of the Pelican case and his dive gear, he probably wouldn't be able to outrun them. Then again, he didn't actually need to outrun them.

"Bones! A little help here!" He spun on his heel and started running back toward the carriage.

With the canopy lowered, Bones' head and shoulders were visible, but Bones wasn't looking forward at Maddock's situation. His focus was on something happening back at the entrance to the street.

"Sorry, dude," Bones replied without turning. "You're gonna have to take a number."

As Maddock wriggled past the caleche, he saw what had arrested Bones' attention. A group of men in *jellabiyahs*—almost certainly the rest of the gang of thieves—were arrayed in a line across the street, blocking the path of escape.

Maddock swore under his breath, but as soon as he was in the open again, he turned and gave the carriage a hard shove. The unexpected jolt took both the driver and the horse by surprise, the latter starting forward as the carriage's traces pushed against its harness. He doubted it would do much to slow the four toughs behind them, but at least it would give him and Bones a little more room to maneuver.

Bones finally glanced over, nodding his approval when he saw that Maddock had recovered the case. "You got her?"

"Yep."

"Good. Now if we can just get past the welcoming committee, we can head to the buffet, and after that, maybe hit the tables, play some Blackjack… Oh, wait. We're not at *that* Luxor."

Maddock ignored the complaint, and nodded his

head down the street. "Blow through these guys?"

Bones' answer took the form of a chant from a childhood game. "Red rover, red rover. Gonna knock your ass over."

On the last syllable, Bones threw back his head and let out a war whoop, then broke into a run, charging headlong toward the human barrier. Summoning up the energy for one more run, Maddock started after him, but no sooner was he moving when the blockade suddenly fell apart. The men scattered, scrambling to get out of the way of a car that had come up from behind them.

A familiar red car, with the distinctive rearing lion logo of the Peugeot automobile company.

Although it wasn't moving very fast by highway speeds, it nevertheless clipped several of the thieves, spinning them out of the way. One man fell across the hood and stayed there, scrambling for something to hold onto as the car began accelerating.

Maddock and Bones both stopped short and then moved aside, pressing themselves against the wall as the sedan approached. When it was almost beside them, the driver slammed on the brakes, catapulting the unlucky hitchhiker down from his tenuous perch on the hood. The man rolled to a stop right in front of the four men from the garage who had succeeded in getting around the carriage. Evidently realizing that the car was there to provide rescue for the two Americans, the men broke into a tentative run.

Beside them, the passenger window began lowering, the Egyptian woman looking out at them, her earlier smile replaced by an urgent, if slightly horrified expression. "What are you waiting for? Get in."

Bones moved first, opening the rear door and

heaving his SCUBA bag inside. He then reached out a hand to Maddock. "Uma!"

Maddock got the message and passed the case back to his friend, then quickly opened the front passenger door and climbed inside. Even before he got the door shut, the woman threw the transmission into reverse and gunned the engine. She continued facing forward, using the mirrors to navigate a surprisingly straight line back down the street. The gang of thieves, who were only just beginning to recover from her arrival, scrambled for the periphery as it became evident that she had no intention of slowing for them or the blind intersection beyond. Maddock, realizing the same thing, braced himself for a possible collision as the sedan broke from the claustrophobic confines of the alley. At the last instant, the woman tapped the brakes and depressed the horn with her thumbs, trumpeting a warning.

The street was empty of vehicle traffic, but several of the caleches were lined up to one side of the turn. The Peugeot shot past them, the woman cranking the steering wheel to the left as soon as they were clear. The sedan swung away in a parabolic curve that ended when the vehicle was aligned with the street and facing back toward the rail crossing. The woman stomped the brake pedal, bringing the vehicle to a screeching halt, then quickly shifted to "drive" and accelerated away again.

The Peugeot sped down the street, slowing just a little at the railroad crossing. As the car rumbled over the tracks, the woman let out her breath in a long, relieved sigh, then glanced over at Maddock and flashed a weak smile. "Welcome to Luxor."

Maddock laughed. "Thanks. And thanks for the assist. That was quite a surprise party. Does that kind of thing happen a lot around here?"

She shook her head. "No. Never. Tourism is very important to the local economy. An attack like this may frighten visitors away, and nobody wants that." She paused a beat. "I suppose you'll want to go to the police station."

There was an odd undercurrent of reluctance in her voice. Ordinarily, Maddock would have preferred to avoid involving the authorities, especially if the attempted theft had been nothing more than a random attack, but the woman's assertion that such crimes were rare gave him pause.

It hadn't really felt like a random or opportunistic action. The attack had been elaborately staged, with several participants all working together in a coordinated effort. And Maddock couldn't shake the feeling that the thieves had specifically targeted them.

But why?

He glanced back at Bones who had the Pelican case open on his lap in order to check for damage. "What do you think?"

"I think I don't want to spend the rest of the day sitting in a police station looking at mug shots. Besides, with our luck, they'd probably lock us up for disturbing the peace and animal cruelty." He snapped the case shut. "Uma's in good shape. No harm, no foul. I say we get on with our day."

Despite his misgivings, Maddock nodded in agreement. "I suppose you're right. We'll tell Dr. Majdy about it. Maybe he'll know what to do."

The woman uttered a short, abrupt laugh.

Maddock shot her an irritated look. "Did I say something funny?"

"'He' is me," she said, grinning. "I am Dr. Majdy. But you must call me Nora."

THREE

"You are Dr. Majdy?" Maddock asked. "Sorry, I just didn't expect—"

"A woman?" Nora finished for him.

"Frankly, yes." Maddock replied.

"Do you have a problem with that?" There was an edge to her voice, but her smile remained. Before he could respond, she continued, "Don't worry. I'm used to it. But I'm as qualified as any male archaeologist in Egypt. Probably more qualified than a lot of them, though try getting any one of them to admit it."

"I don't have a problem with it," he managed, belatedly. "I've worked with several female archaeologists."

From the back seat, Bones gave a snort of laughter. "*Worked* with."

Maddock ignored the jab and tried to choose his words carefully to avoid growing the rift any wider. "It was my understanding that the social climate here is somewhat... Ah..."

"Repressive toward women? It's okay. You can say it. And you're right. It's why I have to wear this thing." She flicked a finger against the fabric of her hijab. "At least when I'm in the city."

The traffic was light—nothing like what Maddock and Bones had seen in Cairo during their brief transit from the airport to the train station—and Dr. Majdy—Nora—drove with an air of casual indifference, changing lanes to avoid carriages and tour buses without any trace of anxiety or hesitation. The shock of the earlier attack seemed already to have faded from her memory.

To their right, the seemingly unbroken wall of

modern concrete buildings abruptly thinned out, revealing trees and a spectacular view of the Nile. Nora stayed on the road as it veered south, paralleling the river though their view of it was partially blocked by several large resort hotels.

"If I'm being perfectly honest," she went on, "That's why I asked for assistance from the Global Heritage Commission, rather than enlisting a local crew. Well, one of the reasons anyway."

"What do you mean?"

She gave him a sidelong glance, then returned her attention to the road, just as the Peugeot entered a traffic circle. She curled the sedan about two-thirds of the way through the roundabout before turning onto another main thoroughfare, this one headed east, away from the river. The urban landscape continued to their right, but to the left lay a broad green field, bordered by more trees. But for the signs written in graceful Arabic script, Maddock might have believed they were in the tropics, rather than one of the hottest, driest places on earth—hotter even than the Sahara Desert

"How much do you know about archaeology in Egypt?"

"Probably not as much as I think I do," Maddock replied. He thought his knowledge on the subject was respectable, but sensed he was about to get schooled.

Bones leaned forward. "I've seen *Raiders of the Lost Ark* about a bajillion times."

Maddock rolled his eyes. *At least he didn't mention The Mummy,* he thought.

He expected Nora to scoff at the reference, but she just nodded. "Exactly my point. Almost all of the significant work was done by foreigners. Maspero.

Flinders Petrie. Howard Carter. Barbara Mertz. And that's still true today because foreign archaeologists have resources that locals don't. The University of Cairo has a world class archaeology program, but the only opportunities for field work are through the Ministry of Antiquities, and they only give permits to their cronies. It's a closed system, mired in bureaucracy. It's bad enough that I'm a woman, but I got my BA and post-graduate degrees in England, which means I'll never be welcome in their clique."

"But you still somehow managed to get a permit?"

For the first time since introducing herself, Nora's smile slipped a little. "Not exactly."

Maddock's wariness returned. Rogue archaeology was fine for fictional characters like Indiana Jones and Lara Croft, but without official sanction, any exploration of a registered archaeological site would be a criminal act—essentially, grave robbing—to which he and Bones would be complicit. "You *do* have a permit?"

"Sort of." She hesitated, pretending to focus on the road, which made a sweeping curve to head southward again. There was no sign of the river now. "It will all make sense when we get where we're going."

Maddock glanced over his shoulder at Bones. His friend gave a helpless shrug and then leaned back as if to enjoy the scenery and began whistling softly. It took Maddock a few seconds to recognize the tune.

Walk Like an Egyptian. Great. Now I'm gonna have that stuck in my head, he thought. He sighed and faced forward again. *What have we gotten ourselves mixed up in?*

They rode along in silence for a while. Though they had

only gone a few miles they had clearly left the urban city center behind. The scenery to either side was now verdant with well-watered fields and groves of palm and citrus trees. The road brought them back to the river, their view now mostly unobstructed as they traveled parallel to its course. Maddock could see several vessels moving in the water—everything from river cruise ships to small lateen-rigged sailboats called *feluccas*. Not too far off, and getting closer with each passing second, a flat girder bridge stretched across the water, providing access to the far shore.

As if sensing an unasked question, Nora broke her silence. "That's where we're going," she said, nodding toward the bridge. "Or across it, rather. To the West Bank."

"To the Valley of the Kings," Maddock supplied, trying to keep the conversation going.

"Eventually, but first we need to make a stop at Deir el-Bahari."

Maddock recalled hearing the name earlier, mentioned by one of the would-be salesman on the train platform, but drew a blank on its significance. "What's that?"

"Forgive me. I forgot that you are not archaeologists."

Maddock couldn't tell if the comment was a thinly-veiled insult or a sincere apology. He decided to believe it was the latter.

"Deir el-Bahari," Nora went on, "is a major mortuary temple complex on the west bank. Very popular with tourists."

That definitely felt like a dig. "We're not here for sightseeing, Dr. Majdy," he said, injecting a little acid into his tone.

"Speak for yourself," Bones interjected. "I wouldn't mind seeing this Derriere el Baja place."

Nora laughed again, though now it seemed a little forced. "Deir el-Bahari," she corrected. "And don't worry. We won't be sightseeing."

The road looped away from the bridge before coming around to meet it. Like the railway station, the divided four-lane bridge was adorned in a faux-Egyptian motif, with a pair of obelisks fronted by large falcon statues, positioned at the gateway. "This bridge was only built about twenty years ago. Before that, the only way to cross was by ferry. Most people still use the ferries, but I like the freedom of having my own car. And it's not that far out of the way."

As they started across it, Maddock was strangely aware of the river below. While he bridled at the thought of being splashed with the "tourist" label, the truth was, he enjoyed traveling to places of historical significance and natural beauty, and the Nile River was certainly both. It was virtually tied with the Amazon for the title of longest river on earth, but unlike the South American river, which flowed through largely untamed jungle, inhabited by tribes of hunter-gatherers, the Nile was inextricably linked to the rise of human civilization. Its flood seasons had brought life to the blistering Egyptian desert for countless millennia. The quest to find its source had inspired some of history's greatest explorers—Livingstone, Stanley, Burton. It was, and perhaps always had been, a symbol of exotic destinations, romance and adventure. Looking at the Nile never failed to spark his imagination and his sense of adventure.

After making the crossing—which took all of about a minute—Nora continued along the highway, heading in a northwesterly direction, almost perpendicular to the river. To either side lay acres of well-watered sugar cane, along with a few signs of human occupation—a mosque, a gas station, stores and houses—but in the distance, rising above the verdant landscape like a cresting wave, was a ridge of bleak sandstone. After about two miles of this, they passed over water again—a pair of irrigation canals—and then turned right at a T-junction, continuing along a tree-lined highway that ran parallel to the canals. The road continued for several miles through the agricultural area before eventually bringing them to a more densely populated area. Here and there, Maddock caught glimpses of the river, and beyond it, the East Bank and Luxor proper. His internal compass told him they had come nearly full-circle; a fifteen-mile detour to bring them back to a point only about a mile or so from where the journey had begun. After another half-mile, Nora took a left turn, heading once more toward the looming desert hills to the west. Signs, printed in both English and Arabic, indicated that they were on the road to Deir el-Bahari and other sites of interest, but even without the signs, Maddock would have guessed that they were close from the increased volume of tour buses and taxis.

"Look there," Nora said, pointing across the dashboard to a pair of objects rising in the foreground. Maddock had already noticed the strange protrusions, which looked like free standing pillars of natural stone, but as they drew closer, he could see that they were in fact carved statues, rising at least fifty feet above ground level. "They are called the Colossi of Memnon," she said.

"Though the statues are actually depictions of Amenhotep III."

"How can you tell?" asked Bones. His question was understandable. Time and weather had blunted the images to the point where they were barely recognizable as seated human figures.

"Though you can't see them from here, there are hieroglyphic inscriptions linking the statues to the reign of Amenhotep which lasted until about 1351 BCE. He was Tutankhamun's grandfather. You can see that the figures are wearing the *nemes* headdress. Only the king would be so depicted."

Maddock squinted up at the statue as they passed, and could definitely distinguish the shape of the traditional Egyptian headgear that looked sort of like a do-rag with flaps hanging down over the shoulders on both sides.

"These statues guarded the entrance to Amenhotep's mortuary temple," she went on. "It was one of the largest ever built. Now, they are all that remain of it."

She glanced over at Maddock with a faintly guilty expression. "Sorry. I know you're not here to play tourist, but talking about this stuff is what I do for a living."

"No apology required," Maddock replied. "It's interesting and it helps to be able to put this stuff into context."

She gave him a grateful smile. "According to folklore, the northern statue was damaged in an earthquake in the year 27 BCE. The quake opened a large crack in the stone, and when the wind blew across it, it produced a distinctive sound which the Greek geographers associated with the cry of the dawn goddess

Eos, mother of the Ethiopian king Memnon—if, that is, you consider the Iliad to be a reliable historical source. They called the statue the Colossus of Memnon, even though it has nothing to do with him, and the name stuck."

"So basically," Bones interjected, "What you're saying is that the statue broke wind from its crack."

Nora pursed her lips together, struggling to suppress an involuntary laugh.

"Maybe I'm the one who should apologize," Maddock said. "For bringing him along."

"Hey, she's the one who said it."

"I said it was folklore," Nora countered, still fighting to maintain her composure. "Nobody knows for certain if the story is true. Sometime during the Second Century, someone—possibly the Roman Emperor Septimus Severus—restored the statue, repairing the earthquake damage. After that, it never …" She broke off, unable to hold back her laughter any longer.

"It never farted again?" Bones supplied.

Shoulders quaking, unshed tears of mirth dancing in her eyes, Nora nodded.

Maddock sighed. "Don't encourage him."

The statues seemed to mark the western limit of the fertile Nile valley. Beyond them, the green fields gave way to bleached desert. The road veered to the right, straddling the border between the two extremes. Here and there, Maddock could see what looked like stone blocks jutting up from the baked earth like broken teeth. Despite the austerity of the landscape, there were signs of human habitation here as well—mostly cafes and gift shops, painted with garish reproductions of Egyptian art.

At the next intersection, Nora made a hard left turn and the Peugeot began a gradual ascent up into the desert foothills, which ended at a large parking lot, half-filled with buses and taxis. Nora slotted the Peugeot into an empty space and switched it off, but before opening her door to exit, she stripped off her hijab, revealing shoulder length black hair.

"That's enough of that," she said, tossing her mane back with a shake of her head. She wore a bright red soccer jersey and black denim jeans. Her bare arms were toned and tan. It occurred to Maddock that none of this had been concealed while she wore the head scarf, but he had not really bothered to look past it.

She noticed his appraising glance and, perhaps mistaking his intent, said, "Don't worry. Out here, I'll blend in a lot better without this." She threw the black scarf onto the center console, then opened her door and got out.

Maddock and Bones got out as well, taking their bags with them. Noticing this, Nora gestured to the rear of the sedan. "You can stow that in the boot if you like."

Bones shook his head. "After what happened back at the train station, there's no way I'm letting this stuff out of my sight."

Nora accepted this without argument, and gestured for them to follow. As they moved across the parking area, Maddock understood Nora's comment about blending in. Aside from a handful of tour guides and gift kiosk operators, there were hardly any Egyptians, and all were male. Everyone else was either Asian or Caucasian, and everyone wore casual Western attire. The only head coverings in evidence were ordinary hats—ball caps, broad-brimmed sun hats, and even a couple felt fedoras.

Had she worn the traditional Muslim head covering, Nora would have immediately attracted unwanted attention, even here in her native country, but without it, even despite her swarthy skin tone and distinctive features, she looked like just another tourist.

At the edge of the parking area, Maddock finally beheld the reason for all the activity. Nestled against the base of the high sandstone bluff was a broad multi-tiered structure that looked to be at least as long as a football field. Each tier was fronted by perfectly spaced columns. A long ramp took them from ground level to a courtyard on the second tier, and halfway across it, another ramp ascended to the third, letting out onto a broad colonnaded balcony overlooking the complex. The interior of the third level was evidently off limits, the space between the pillars blocked with a wire fence, but there was still plenty to see without going in. Maddock immediately noted a detail that hadn't been visible from a distance. Statues had once stood guard in front of the tall columns supporting the roof. A few still remained. The standing figures, which were nearly twice his own height, looked virtually identical. They reminded Maddock of pictures he had seen of King Tut's coffin, with the same kind of exaggerated beards, arms crossed over the chest in the traditional funerary pose and holding the crook and flail—traditional symbols of ruling power—but there were differences, too. Instead of the flap-like head covering—the *nemes,* Nora had called it—these figures wore a tall crown that looked almost like a bowling pin. The face was broader, the cheeks plump, almost feminine, something Bones did not fail to notice. As they stepped off onto the broad porch in front of the colonnade, he gestured to the nearest statue.

"Dude looks like a lady."

"Dude *is* a lady," Nora replied. "Or was. This is the mortuary temple of Hatshepsut, one of the greatest rulers in Egyptian history. And yes, she was a *she*."

"What was that name again?" Bones said.

"Hatshepsut."

"One more time."

Maddock could see the wheels turning in his friend's head, and took preemptive action. "Bones, knock it off." He turned to Nora. "So what's her story?"

"Hatshepsut was the daughter of Thutmose I and his queen Ahmose. The previous ruler, Amenhotep—"

"The farting guy?" Bones asked.

"No, that was Amenhotep III. He came later. Amenhotep I died without a male heir, so a lesser prince—Thutmose I—took the throne by marrying Amenhotep's daughter, Ahmose. Bloodlines were very important to the Egyptians, partly as a legal basis for transfer of power, but mostly because the king was supposed to be a living god, and his children—male or female—would have divine blood. Thutmose had a son by one of his other wives, but because Hatshepsut had the stronger blood claim, she and her half-brother, Thutmose II, were married. Most scholars believe she was probably the power behind the throne during his reign, which might have only lasted three or four years, depending on who you ask. Thutmose II died when Thutmose III—his only son by another of his wives— was only two years old, so while he was technically the heir, she had a stronger claim to the throne, and since she was probably already the de facto ruler, she took the added step of declaring herself the actual ruler."

"I take it that was unusual," said Maddock. "A

female actually taking the title of pharaoh?"

"Strictly speaking, the term 'pharaoh' wasn't used to refer to the king until around 1200 BCE. We just sort of retroactively apply it to all the rulers before that. But the symbols in surviving inscriptions, as well as the presence of crowns and the royal beard in the statuary, indicate that she was not merely filling in but considered herself the actual king of Egypt.

"She wasn't the first female ruler, but she was certainly the first to make an impression on history. One Egyptologist called her 'the first great woman in history of whom we are informed.' And it wasn't just because she was a woman in a man's job. She was one of the most successful rulers in Egyptian history, and certainly the most successful of the Eighteenth Dynasty."

She pronounced the word in typical British fashion, with a soft 'y' and the first syllable break after the 'n.' Maddock couldn't resist making a comment, stressing the American pronunciation. "I've never actually understood all these references to dynasties."

"Dynasties," she corrected, flashing him a wry grin. "Well, I'll try to give you the short version, but you have to remember that what we call the Ancient Egyptian civilization lasted nearly three thousand years. As my first history professor was fond of saying, that's a bloody long time. They had their ups and downs, like anyone would, but generally speaking there are three distinct periods—we call them Kingdoms. The Old Kingdom, from about 2686 BCE to 2181 BCE, was ruled from Memphis, near modern day Cairo."

"This is all screwed up," Bones said, but with a mischievous twinkle in his eye. "First Luxor isn't in Vegas anymore, and now you tell me Memphis isn't in

Tennessee?"

"Where do you think they got the idea for that? What better name for the jewel of the American Nile."

"I guess that means Elvis wasn't just the King. He was Pharaoh, too."

"That's a bit too far outside my field. At any rate, the Old Kingdom was the age of the pyramid builders and comprised the Third through the Sixth Dynasties—that is to say, distinct royal lines. The Old Kingdom collapsed during a century long global drought event, which actually wiped out several early human civilizations in Europe and Asia. We don't really know much about that intermediate period which isn't really surprising since monumental building projects weren't exactly a high priority, what with everyone starving. But eventually things turned around during the reign of Mentuhotep II of the Eleventh Dynasty. He reunified Upper and Lower Egypt, and that began the period we call the Middle Kingdom, which lasted almost four hundred years, until about 1650 BCE, and comprised the Eleventh through Thirteenth Dynasties. Even though this was a more prosperous time, we have very little physical documentation from the Middle Kingdom, or from the other dynasties during the second intermediate period. But it was during this period that the power began to shift to Upper Egypt, and by the time of the New Kingdom, and the Eighteenth Dynasty, this—" She waved a hand in an expansive gesture. "Was the center of the world. And that was mainly due to Hatshepsut. She re-established trade routes to neighboring kingdoms, which greatly increased Egypt's wealth, and commissioned hundreds of building projects, including this temple. As impressive as it is today, just imagine what it would have looked like in the time of Hatshepsut. We call it her mortuary temple, but I think its original name—Djeser-Djeseru, the Sublime of Sublimes—is far more evocative."

"It's a nice place," Bones said with a shrug, "But it's no pyramid."

Nora rolled her eyes. "Pyramids are boring. I'd take this over a pyramid any day of the week."

"Yeah, but they're big."

"Bigger isn't always better," she retorted.

Bones elbowed Maddock. "Hear that, dude? There's hope for you after all."

Maddock ignored the all-too familiar ribbing. "So why isn't she more famous? I mean, aside from the fact that her name is kind of hard to remember. I've heard of other Egyptian queens. Nefertiti. Cleopatra. Why don't more people know about Queen Hat?"

"King Hat," Nora corrected. "There were lots of queens, but Hatshepsut ruled as if she was actually king. But to answer your question, part of the reason is political. At some point after her death, someone—either her son Thutmose III or his son, Amenhotep II—did his best to erase her completely from history. Her name was chiseled off royal cartouches. Many of her statues were torn down and thrown into landfills. Even here."

She gestured to the next pillar in line, in front of which there was just the base of a statue and what appeared to be a pair of disconnected feet. Maddock realized that there were similar broken bases in front of most of the other pillars on the same level.

"Just because she was a woman?"

"Not necessarily. It was a common practice in ancient times for kings to remove all mention of their predecessors as a way of increasing their own prestige. Given the scope of her accomplishments, its not surprising that the men who came after might have felt a little threatened."

Maddock did not fail to note the subtext, but Nora quickly moved on.

"There were also some major political and cultural shifts that may have played a role later on. About a century after Hatshepsut, Amenhotep IV created a new religion worshipping Aten, the sun disk. He changed his name to Akhenaten and built a new capital city in Amarna, about halfway between here and Memphis."

Maddock started a little in surprise at the mention of Akhenaten. A few years earlier, he and Bones, along with his former girlfriend, archaeologist Jade Ihara, had discovered the shocking truth about the so-called "heretic" pharaoh. He tried to cover his reaction with a more innocuous question. "I thought the Egyptians were already worshipping the sun at that time."

"Think of it more as a sectarian revolution. Aten was an aspect of Amun Re, so it wasn't as if Akhenaten was introducing a new deity. Rather, he was claiming that he had special knowledge of how the deity was to be worshipped. All religions grow out of earlier traditions. Judaism, Christianity and Islam all worship the God of Abraham, but each one insists that they have received the correct revelation of how he ought to be worshipped, and within each, there are sectarian differences."

Bones, who had been looking around, seemingly oblivious to the lecture, now spoke up. "I read somewhere that Akhenaten might have been Moses."

Maddock winced and shot his friend a warning glance. Nora just gawped at him. "Moses? As in the

Exodus?" She shook her head. "That's preposterous. In any case, the Exodus account isn't history. Period." She shook her head again as if trying to remove all traces of the idea from her head. "You mentioned Nefertiti. We actually know even less about her than Hatshepsut—"

"I know that she was a babe," Bones put in.

Nora pushed on. "She was Akhenaten's queen, and had a great deal of influence over him. Recent discoveries have suggested that she also may have served as co-regent, and like Hatshepsut, ruled as king, using the name Neferneferuaten. During her reign, power shifted back to Thebes and the so-called Aten heresy ended. When Akhenaten's son Tutankhaten, took the throne, he changed his name to—"

"Tutankhamun," Maddock finished, nodding in understanding. "So Nefertiti was Tut's mother?"

Nora seemed pleased that he had put it all together. "His biological mother died in childbirth, but Nefertiti raised the boy and probably continued serving as regent until her death.

"As you probably know, Tutankhamun's reign did not last long—maybe just ten years—and he was constantly at odds with his vizier, Ay, and the general of his armies, Horemheb. When he died—and some believe he was murdered—both men eventually succeeded him to the throne, and Horemheb, who was not of royal blood, purged almost all mention of his predecessors. That was it for the Eighteenth Dynasty."

"How many more are there?" Bones said.

"Strictly speaking, there are thirty-three distinct ruling dynasties—if you include the Argean and Ptolemaic Dynasties."

"Thirty-three?" Bones groaned. He checked his

watch. "So, we're barely halfway. Maybe we can take a break for lunch? I think I saw a sign for Mickey-D's back in Luxor."

"Sorry," Nora said. "I tend to get a little carried away. Suffice it to say, the third period—the New Kingdom—reached its zenith with the Nineteenth Dynasty, and specifically during the reign of Ramesses the Great which ended in 1213 BCE. By the end of the Twentieth Dynasty in 1077, the Empire had effectively collapsed and many of those who took the title Pharaoh after that were foreigners—Libyans, Nubians, Persians, Greeks. The last person to be called 'pharaoh' was Ptolemy XV, the son of Cleopatra and Julius Caesar, but he never really ruled over anything. And no, that won't be on the test. As for lunch... There's something I have to take care of first. Follow me."

FOUR

She led them along the colonnade toward the north end of the balcony to a gated opening in the security fence. The gate was closed but an Egyptian man in Western attire was positioned just inside, guarding the entrance. Nora approached and said something in Arabic. Maddock had learned a few phrases in the language during his time in the military, but the only words he recognized now were names. Nora's and someone else. Mohamed something.

The gatekeeper regarded her with an irritated and faintly suspicious expression, but then his gaze moved to Maddock and Bones, and after appraising them for a moment, he replied in the same language and then opened the gate to admit them.

Nora led them through the tightly spaced columns but paused at the edge of a sunlit interior courtyard. Maddock was surprised to see what looked like a small tour group gathered in a loose semi-circle in the middle of the open area, their backs turned to the entrance. He assumed that they must be academics—archaeologists like Nora, which probably explained how she had been able to gain access to the restricted area—but on closer examination, he realized that one of the men was standing behind a tripod mounted video camera. Another man had a slightly smaller shoulder mounted camera trained in the same general direction, and yet another was holding a boom microphone over the heads of the others in the group. The half-circle blocked his view of the subject, but Bones evidently had a better angle.

"Dude, do you know who that is?"

A couple of heads turned to look at him, fingers raised to lips in the universal gesture for 'shut the hell up.' Bones ignored them. "That's Max Riddle. He must be filming for his show."

The name meant nothing to Maddock, but knowing Bones' television viewing habits, he could hazard a guess. "Aliens or cryptids?"

Bones grinned, his answer confirming that Maddock was on the right track. "Max used to work with Jo Slater."

That was a name Maddock did recognize. Joanne Slater was the star of *Expedition: Adventure*, a cable TV documentary series about the search for mythic monsters, ghosts, lost treasures, and pretty much anything else that couldn't be definitively proven to exist. Bones wasn't just a fan of Slater's show; he had actually joined her on an expedition to search for Florida's legendary Skunk Ape.

"I guess they'll give anyone a TV show these days," Bones went on. "Maybe we should look into that. Don't worry about your face though. You can just do the voice overs." He gave a snort of laughter, which earned him another, more vigorous round of shushing from the production crew, and then someone from the group yelled. "Cut."

Now, all eyes in the group turned to glare at them, and Maddock could see the two men who had, until that moment, been the focus of attention. The younger of the pair was tall and broad, with a face that, despite its present irritated frown, looked perpetually cheerful. Maddock guessed that had to be Riddle. The other man—older, shorter, grumpier—had the dark complexion and striking features of an Egyptian. He wore a leather vest over a vividly blue long sleeve work shirt and a weathered fedora, pushed back just far enough to reveal bushy white eyebrows. Maddock was certain that he recognized this man from somewhere.

Rather than chiding Bones for interrupting the filming, Nora immediately charged forward toward the group. As she drew close, the older man's eyes narrowed to focus on her, and his already irked expression deepened into real anger. "You!"

"Dr. Zahi," Nora said, with unexpected pleasantness. "I was hoping to find you here."

Given the purposefulness she had earlier exhibited, Maddock knew the words were disingenuous. Nora had known exactly where this Dr. Zahi would be, and had timed her visit accordingly. The utterance of the name provided the clue Maddock had needed to solving the mystery of why the man looked familiar. This was Dr. Zahi Mohamed, the self-styled Egyptian Indiana Jones, and presently the head of the Egyptian government's Ministry of Antiquities. Although his scholarly qualifications were well-established, Maddock knew the man had a reputation as a glory-hound. He was a fixture on cable television documentaries, and not just the ones that focused on real history and hard archaeology, though to his credit, when the subject matter veered into extreme speculation—as it all too often seemed to do in Egypt—he was usually consulted as the contrary voice of reason.

Earlier, when Nora had been bemoaning the stifling bureaucracy of the Ministry of Antiquities, it hadn't really dawned on Maddock that the source of the problem was this would-be celebrity archaeologist.

A glance at the cameramen confirmed Maddock's

suspicion that, despite the "cut" order, they were still shooting, probably hoping that this interruption of the scripted interview might lead to something even more exciting. It was, after all, supposed to be "reality" television. Nora had almost certainly factored that into her ambush as well.

"I am quite busy," Zahi said, with a disdainful sniff. "If you wish to speak with me, contact my office and make an appointment."

Beside him, Max Riddle's gaze settled on Nora, and his frown evaporated. He stepped forward, making sure to position himself so the camera would keep him framed, and thrust out a hand. "Hi. I'm Max Riddle, host of *Maximum Mysteries.*"

Bones quickly stepped in front of him and seized the outstretched hand. "Max, dude. Great to meet you. So what are you looking for? Let me guess. Proof that aliens built the pyramids?"

Riddle stared up at the big man warily but managed to sustain his smile. "Not this time. Actually, I'm investigating the Mystery of the Dendera Light. We're just getting some background here, but we'll be heading up to Dendera this afternoon." He paused a beat, then his gaze narrowed. "You do know about the Dendera Light, don't you?"

Bones shook his head. "Nah, but she probably does." He cocked his head over his shoulder to indicate Nora.

As if on cue, Nora slipped around Bones. "How do you do? I'm Dr. Nora Majdy. I'm so sorry to have interrupted your filming, but this is an urgent matter. It will only take a moment."

Zahi shook his head and waved an emphatic hand. "No. No. You'll have to make an appointment."

"Well, now I'm curious," Riddle said, his smile now turned up to full intensity. "And I'm sure my viewers would like to hear more about this... Whatever it is."

As if suddenly realizing what Nora was attempting, Zahi stepped forward quickly, forcing a smile for the cameras. "What I meant to say, Dr. Majdy—" He said it through clenched teeth, stressing both her title and name in a way that seemed almost menacing. "—is that a matter this sensitive should be discussed in a less public setting."

"How 'bout over there?" Bones said, hooking a thumb toward the corner of the courtyard.

Nora registered mild surprise at his suggestion, but then immediately nodded. "That's fine with me," she said, and then, with a grateful smile to Bones, started walking in the indicated direction as if Zahi had already acceded. After a quick glance toward the cameras, the older archaeologist mumbled, "This won't take a moment," and then went after her.

Bones glanced at Maddock and cocked his head in their direction, the unasked question easily interpreted. Maddock nodded, and they both followed.

Now safely out of view of the cameras, Zahi allowed his mask of civility to slip away. He regarded Nora with an expression of pure contempt, and then, realizing that Maddock and Bones were there as well, gave them the same treatment. "This is a private discussion," he hissed.

"It's okay," Bones said. "We're with her."

Nora however adopted a more conciliatory tone. "Dr. Zahi, please forgive me. I did try to make an appointment with—"

"What do you want?" he snapped, clearly uninterested in smoothing things over.

"As I'm sure you've probably heard, we found something interesting in the West Valley."

"We? Who is 'we'? Certainly not you. I know for a fact that you don't have permission to be digging in the West Valley, or anywhere else, for that matter."

"Dr. Majdy has been working at my behest," said a calm voice from behind Maddock. The speaker, who had been standing with the production crew, was a handsome looking Egyptian man who looked to be about the same age as Maddock. He wore dress slacks and a white business shirt, open at the collar, and as he approached the small group, he offered a warm smile and an open hand to Maddock. "How do you do? I am Nassir Fayed."

Like Nora, he spoke flawless English with just a hint of a British accent. Maddock accepted the handclasp, which was firmer than he had anticipated, but before he could introduce himself, Zahi spoke up. "She is working for you, Fayed? I don't understand."

Fayed still gripping Maddock's hand, said, "You will have to forgive Dr. Zahi. He is very protective of our great culture, and sometimes forgets his manners. I think it comes from spending too much time with dead people, and not enough with the living."

Zahi glared at the younger man. "So this is why you wished to accompany me today." The subdued tone of the accusation spoke volumes about the power dynamic between the two men.

Maddock nodded to the newcomer, and said simply, "I'm Dane Maddock. This is my partner, Mr. Bonebrake. Dr. Majdy invited us here to help with some underwater survey work." He paused a beat. "But I guess if she's working for you, then you already know all about that."

"I do," Fayed said. "But, it would not be accurate to say that Dr. Majdy is working *for* me. I am…" He tilted his eyes up, as if searching for the word. "Sponsoring the excavation."

"Sponsoring?" Maddock wondered if the carefully chosen words were concealing an indiscreet relationship. Normally, he wouldn't have cared—it was none of his business what people he barely knew did with their private lives—but he had already had enough drama for one day, and didn't want to get dragged into the middle of an Egyptian soap opera. "You *are* an archaeologist?"

"I'm an enthusiast, Mr. Maddock. A well-connected one, at that." He glanced over at Zahi, grinning. "From time to time, I finance expeditions of discovery, and help smooth out some of the obstacles in the permitting process." He paused a beat before adding, "I believe I am also providing lodging for you and your associate."

"Mr. Fayed owns a very successful resort hotel here in Luxor," Nora said, speaking in a low, unobtrusive voice, like a language interpreter. Maddock detected no embarrassment or deception in her voice. Whatever else their relationship was, it didn't appear to be romantic in nature.

"Archaeological discoveries are as much the life blood of my city as the Nile," Fayed said, with an expansive air. "Luxor has been called 'the world's greatest open-air museum.' But even the best museum must, from time to time, add new pieces to the collection. Without that, people lose interest. Visitors stop coming and the city withers and dies."

"Archaeology is the quest to learn about our history," Zahi muttered, refusing to meet Fayed's gaze. "Not entertain tourists."

Fayed did not comment on the obvious hypocrisy of the statement, but continued speaking. "And we have the added problem of religious extremists, who have from time to time, targeted visitors from the West. One of the worst incidents happened right here in this remarkable place. Twenty years ago. I was a young man then, but I remember it like it was yesterday. Sixty-two people murdered. Shot and hacked to death with machetes. We have never recovered from that, and no matter what steps we may take to protect our guests, every year, fewer people come. The fear of what may happen keeps them away. We must change that perception, Mr. Maddock. Remind the world that this is a place of discovery, not violence. So, you see, it is in my best interests to facilitate new discoveries, and to cultivate the next generation of rising stars in the field of Egyptology." He smiled at Nora. "I see a bright future for Dr. Majdy."

Maddock nodded in understanding. If Zahi Mohamed was Egypt's Indiana Jones, then Fayed was grooming Nora to be its Lara Croft—a female treasure hunter for the next generation. Vivacious and telegenic, Nora would certainly play well on the world stage, but in the increasingly fundamentalist climate of Egypt, it would be a tough sell.

He turned to Nora. "So then you *do* have permission?"

"As I told you," Nora said, some of her earlier hesitancy returning. "It's a little complicated. The permit Mr. Fayed secured for my excavation is limited in scope."

"Limited how?"

"Physically. You see, the plots in the Valley of the Kings are divided up, much like parcels of land. My permit allows me to explore only so far."

"And since that well might lead somewhere beyond the boundaries, you need additional permission to explore it."

She nodded, and then turned to Zahi, deferential once again. "Obviously, I would not dream of jeopardizing my claim to the site, to say nothing of my career, by pushing ahead without the permission of the Ministry of Antiquities. But this is a significant discovery. We have never found anything like this. Who knows what it may lead to? We should not wait to begin surveying it."

As if remembering the power he held, Zahi straightened and shook his head. "I'm sorry, but this is not a simple thing."

"Why not?" Bones interjected. "You're the boss, aren't you?"

"Well, I—Yes, but—"

"Zahi," Fayed said, almost crooning. "You don't want people thinking that you are standing in the way of progress, do you?" He gave an almost imperceptible nod toward the production crew. A quick glance told Maddock that the cameras were still rolling. Even if the audio equipment didn't pick up their conversation, body language would speak volumes.

Zahi opened his mouth to speak, then closed it again with a frown. He sighed. "And just what do you think you will find down there?"

Nora shot a glance at Fayed, and after receiving a nod, returned her attention to Zahi. "The entrance to the site lies just to the southeast of WV 23, on the opposite side of the wadi. The well is being fed by the Nile, which might indicate an underwater passage leading all the way back to the river. There may be other wells, tapping the same underground river, that remain undiscovered."

The description meant nothing to Maddock, but Zahi seemed to immediately understand. "You believe it may also lead to undiscovered tombs."

Nora hesitated again, but Maddock sensed a barely restrained eagerness to share an amazing revelation. "It's really too soon to speculate without more information."

"You must give me something to go on," Zahi persisted.

Nora lowered her gaze, refusing to meet his stare. "Yes, I think the underwater passage may connect to other tombs. Tombs that we have believed lost to history."

Zahi seemed to genuinely consider this for a moment, but then shook his head. "No. You are chasing shadows."

Maddock spoke up. "Then what harm is there in letting us do the survey?"

"What harm?" Zahi's eyes flicked toward Riddle and his production crew. "Only that you would make us all look foolish."

"Really, Zahi," Fayed murmured. "We're not proposing to do this in front of television cameras. All we are proposing is that you let us survey this well with a robot camera. If Dr. Majdy's team finds something, we can revisit the issue of the permit."

Maddock sensed that, regardless of Zahi's feelings, the issue was already settled. The elder archaeologist signaled his displeasure with a long silence, but then inclined his head. "I will allow that your permit may extend to this hypothetical underground river passage, but if you should happen to find the entrance to another structure, that is another matter entirely. I won't have you rushing into an unspoiled tomb."

"Of course not." Nora bowed her head. "Thank you—"

Zahi had already turned away, stalking back to rejoin the Maximum Mysteries production team. Nora shifted her attention back to Fayed. "And thank you."

"He really is a dinosaur," Fayed replied, his gaze following Zahi. Then he clapped his hands together softly and turned to Nora. "When will you begin?"

Nora silently handed the question over to Maddock with a glance. "We're good to go when you are," Maddock said.

"After lunch," Bones added.

"Well then," Fayed said, "Don't let me keep you. Good hunting."

FIVE

"So I guess that's a no to McDonalds," Bones grumbled.

Maddock shook his head, taking the sandwich from the vendor operating his food cart in the marketplace at the edge of the parking area. Nora had called them sandwiches; he would have called them "wraps"—local Egyptian bread, which looked sort of like a pita, stuffed with cucumbers, tomatoes, and some kind of meat that smelled delicious, all wrapped in a piece of newspaper. He nodded graciously to the man, and recalling the Arabic word for "thank you," said, "*Shukran*,"

He then turned to Bones. "McDonald's? Really?"

"Hey, not just McDonalds. Egyptian McDonalds. I could really go for a Big Tut with large… Uh… Fries." Bones grabbed two of the sandwiches, offering one of them to Nora who had already paid for their fare, along with several bottles of water. She declined with an absent wave of the hand.

"Don't get me wrong," Bones went on. "I'm fine with this… Whatever it is. I just don't want word to get out that I'm eating hipster crap."

Maddock wagged his head in disbelief. "How is this hipster food?"

"Dude, you need to get out more. All those man-bun Birkenstock-wearing douches are into street food these days." His protestations notwithstanding, he proceeded to peel back the edge of the paper and took a bite, the size of which indicated no reluctance whatsoever. "Not bad," he muttered through a mouthful.

"If you behave yourself," Nora said, "I will take you to McDonald's for supper. But it is all the way back in Luxor. Valley of the Kings is only a few miles from here."

She was staring across the parking lot, as if eager to keep moving.

"Hey, what was that thing Max was talking about?" Bones asked. "Dander… Dender… Some kind of light?"

It took a moment for Nora to realize he was addressing her. Her gaze refocused and she turned to look at him. "Dendera Light."

"Yeah, what is that? Sounds like a UFO or something?"

She shook her head. "It's nothing. Wishful thinking on the part of people who know nothing of Egyptology." She sighed. "On the walls of the temple of Hathor in Dendera, there are three relief images that show a *djed* pillar—that's a sort of column with four horizontal lines at its top—supporting a bubble of some kind that is growing out of a lotus flower. Inside the bubble is a snake. To those who are ignorant of Egyptian art or mythology, the bubble looks like an electric light bulb, and the snake is the filament, which to their way of thinking, proves that the ancient Egyptians learned the secret of creating electric light three thousand years before Thomas Edison."

Bones snapped his fingers. "Holy crap. I remember reading about that. It was on a website about alien technology in the ancient world. It was all about the Tulli Papyrus."

Nora made a noise that sounded a little like a growl. When she spoke again, she seemed to be clenching her teeth. "Leaving aside the fact that the meaning of the Dendera reliefs is quite evident to anyone with even a simple grasp of Egyptian creation myths, there is no physical evidence to indicate that the ancient Egyptians possessed the means to create an electrical power network or vacuum tubes or any of the other things that would be necessary to produce and actually use a single light bulb."

Sensing that Bones' other fringe theories might not be well received, Maddock hastened to change the subject. "What are the undiscovered tombs you mentioned to Dr. Zahi?"

Nora gazed back at him for a moment, as if weighing how much to reveal, then gestured with her water bottle toward the parking lot. "I'll tell you on the way."

Both men finished their sandwiches before reaching the car and started swigging water as Nora drove the Peugeot back down the hill road. In no time at all, they were heading north on an unfamiliar road that curved back up into the hills before winding west again. As before, the two-way stream of buses and taxis indicated that their next destination was also a tourist attraction, albeit a less popular one than Deir El-Bahari. The ride was brief, lasting no more than ten minutes, and ended at a small disembarkation area, but instead of finding a parking spot, Nora turned onto a small dirt road, blocked by a metal gate. After a quick exchange with the guard posted there, the gate was opened, allowing them to continue up the road, which led into a narrow canyon—the local term, Maddock knew was *wadi*—which cut through the towering sandstone bluffs to either side. In a matter of seconds, the parking lot was lost from view. The primitive road surface forced Nora to slow the car to a crawl. After negotiating several sinuous curves, she finally pulled the Peugeot to the side of the road, opposite a junction with a side road that looked too narrow to accommodate a vehicle. "We'll have to walk the rest of the way," she said, opening her door. "But it's only about two hundred meters."

She circled to the rear of the car and opened the trunk, taking out a small backpack which she slung over one shoulder. Maddock and Bones got out, hefting their burdens, and proceeded to follow her up a winding trail into a smaller wadi. The walls of the ravine rose up to either side, As they walked, Nora launched into her promised explanation.

"Back there is the main complex called Valley of the Kings," she said. "That is where most of the major discoveries were made, including the tomb of Tutankhamun. This area is West Valley, which was a later addition to the necropolis. There are only four major tomb excavations in here, and one of them was never used."

"Why not?" Bones asked. "Dude forgot to die?"

"The tomb was never finished. It is generally believed that it was meant for Akhenaten, and commissioned by Tutankhamun himself. Akhenaten built a Royal Necropolis in Amarna, and when he died, he was buried there along with several members of his family, but when Tutankhamun restored the throne to Thebes, he ordered the remains of Akhenaten and the others to be reburied in the Valley of the Kings, close to his own tomb. Planning one's own funeral was a very important part of Egyptian life, even for someone as young as Tutankhamun. But he died before the task could be completed, and in the subsequent confusion, those plans went awry. Ay, Tut's successor, was buried here in the West Valley, but there is some evidence to suggest Ay may have appropriated the tomb Tutankhamun had commissioned for himself, and had Tut placed in the smaller tomb that was originally meant for Ay."

"What an asshat," Bones muttered.

"You must remember that Tutankhamun died suddenly at a young age. His tomb may not have been finished at the time. It is also interesting to note that some of the funerary objects found in Tut's tomb seem to have originally been buried with Neferneferuaten."

"Who might actually have been Nefertiti," Maddock said, recalling the earlier story.

"Exactly."

"Reduce, reuse, recycle," Bones commented. "But why even bother? Dude is dead. Long live the new dude."

"Dead or not, Tut was still considered a god. Ay may have been a distant relative—we're not sure about that—but his claim to the throne was weak. He couldn't afford to publicly repudiate Tutankhamun. Not at first, anyway. To consolidate his power, Ay married Tutankhamun's queen—and half-sister—Ankhesenamun—"

"Geez," Bones said. "Game of Thrones has nothing on these guys."

Nora smiled. "You have no idea. It is possible that, before she married Tut, Ankhesenamun was the consort of her own father, Akhenaten. Like I told you, royal blood was very important to the Egyptians. Just like Nefertiti and Hatshepsut, Ankhesenamun was the full-blooded daughter of the king and his royal wife. And if Nefertiti had actually ruled as king, then Ankhesenamun was daughter of not one but two divine personages.

"In any case, Ay was able to take power through his marriage to Ankhesenamun, so it was essential for him to at least give the appearance of honoring the rulers who came before, but he clearly wasn't interested in sharing power with her, or she with him. She may have tried to broker a marriage with a Hittite prince named Zannanza, but he died on his way to meet her, and Ankhesenamun herself died not long after. Probably murdered on orders from Ay. Once she was out of the way, Ay had no incentive to honor the line of Akhenaten. We don't know with certainty what became of the remains of Akhenaten, Nefertiti, Ankhesenamun, or the others."

Now Maddock understood. "You think the well might lead to their tombs."

He decided to omit the fact that he and Bones had seen the mummified remains of Akhenaten and Nefertiti with their own eyes, not in the Egyptian desert, but in the American Southwest. Maybe they weren't here, but that didn't mean Nora's underlying premise was wrong.

Nora grimaced, as if afraid that answering in the affirmative might jinx the endeavor. "In Egyptian mythology, Ra, the sun god, travels across the sky during the day on a royal barge called *Mandjet*—the morning boat. But at night, after sunset, he travels through the Underworld on *Mesektet*—the evening boat. It is no coincidence that the necropolis lies to the west of the Nile, where the sun sets. The Egyptians believed the entrance to the Underworld lay to the west, and in their belief system, the Underworld is an underground river."

"So if someone, a tomb builder, accidentally discovered an underground river, he might have believed it was an actual passage to the afterlife."

"I do not believe it would have been interpreted literally," Nora said quickly. "But I do believe that Tutankhamun's architect, Sennedjem, might have recognized both the symbolic and practical potential of a subterranean waterway."

"Practical?"

"The ancient Egyptians believed that disturbing the remains of the dead could harm the soul of the departed in the afterlife. They went to extraordinary lengths to protect the tombs, especially those of the pharaohs."

"Like with booby traps," Bones said. "And curses."

Nora chuckled. "Not quite. The tomb builders relied on secrecy more than anything else, hiding the location of the entrances so that looters would not be able to find their way inside. I'm afraid curses and booby traps are only found in movies and very bad action adventure novels."

Bones shot Maddock a knowing look, then pressed his case. "You're kidding, right? Everybody knows about the curse of King Tut's tomb."

"Sorry to disappoint you, but I'm afraid that's a bit of unsubstantiated folklore. The notion of a curse upon those who entered Tut's tomb was largely based on a combination of hysteria and coincidence."

"That's what skeptics always say. But I don't believe in coincidences. One or two deaths from accidents, maybe, but something like eight or nine of the people who went into Tut's tomb died."

Nora cocked an eyebrow at him. "Actually, all of them died."

"You know what I mean. They died within a year of the tomb being opened. And they weren't just car accidents and natural causes. Some of them were never explained."

The archaeologist sighed as if the all-too familiar subject had become wearisome. "People die, Bones. Despite what you've heard, every single incident associated with the so-called 'curse' has a rational explanation. But what nobody ever talks about is the fact that there was no curse on the sealed entrance to the tomb. There are a few examples of tomb curses from the Old Kingdom, but nothing like that was found on Tut's tomb or anywhere else in the Valley. The whole notion of a 'curse' was invented by Sir Arthur Conan Doyle, who I might add, also believed in fairies."

Before Bones could protest, Maddock intervened. "You were saying something about Tut's architect?"

"Yes. Forgive me. All this talk of curses…" She shuddered, and then gestured ahead to the end of the wadi, where several piles of recently disturbed earth were heaped up at the base of one wall. "As I told you earlier, owing to the purges of Ay and Horemheb, much of the history of the Eighteenth Dynasty is incomplete, but it appears that Tutankhamun's chief tutor—a man named Sennedjem—was also the architect of his royal tomb, and perhaps was commissioned to carve out tombs for Tut's family as well. I think he conceived of a tomb that would be truly impossible for thieves to reach."

She paused as they reached the edge of the excavation and slipped off her backpack. As she dug into its contents, Maddock got his first look at the narrow opening cut into the cliff wall. It was barely wide enough to accommodate one person, the ceiling so low that even Nora would have to duck her head to pass.

"Here," she said, handing each of them a disposable paper respirator mask. "You'll want to wear this once we go inside."

Bones regarded the mask suspiciously. "Why? Is it dangerous?"

"No more dangerous than the Curse of the

Pharaohs," Nora replied with a grin. Then, more soberly, she went on. "Ordinarily, we wouldn't need such a precaution, but the moisture from the well has caused the growth of a black mold fungus. There's not a great deal of it, but better safe than sorry." She tilted her head sideways, looking at Bones. "You know, some believe that mold spores might have contributed to the rumors of the curse."

"You just said there was no curse," retorted Bones.

"And there wasn't. But there may be something to the idea, nevertheless. Mold spores can cause a wide array of health problems—everything from respiratory distress to erratic, even violent behavior. It's not impossible that some of the so-called 'victims' of the curse may have been exposed to mold spores, or some other pathogen that had been dormant in the tomb." She held up another mask and grinned again. "That is why we take precautions."

After fitting the mask in place, she took out a large flashlight, clicked it on, and pointed it into the depths. "Follow me."

While Bones continued staring at the mask in his hand like it was a snake, Maddock donned his and headed into the narrow slot.

The passage descended for about fifty feet on stairs cut out of the surrounding sedimentary rock. The close confines allowed little light from the surface to penetrate the depths—even less once Bones finally overcame his hesitancy to bring up the rear. Nor could Maddock see very much looking forward since Nora's body blocked his view, and most of the illumination from her flashlight. He wasn't normally claustrophobic, but enclosed spaces like this triggered a natural wariness, especially in the near-total absence of light. The weird sound of his own breathing, restricted and distorted by the respirator, did little to ease his anxiety. The tightness of the mask, covering mouth and nose, left him with the sensation of being smothered. With an effort, he suppressed these primal fears, and focused on putting one foot in front of the next.

The staircase fed into a gently sloping passage which continued in the same direction for another fifty feet or so, then there were more stairs, wending ever deeper into the hillside. The descent continued in this fashion, with several more long flights of carved steps, interspersed with flat and gently sloping sections that might have been intended as galleries or even crypts for the Pharaohs, but always the downward journey continued. The air was both cool and stifling, particularly with the partial obstruction of the mask, and Maddock was grateful for Nora's moderate pace.

Finally, after about ten minutes of travel, the passage opened up wide enough to permit all three of them to walk abreast. No sooner had it done this, than the passage dead-ended, but set in the middle of the cul-de-sac at its terminus was a round opening about ten feet across.

Nora strode to its edge and played her light down into it, revealing a cylindrical pit descending even deeper. A staircase, barely a foot wide, had been cut into the side of the pit to spiral around its outer edge, descending well beyond the reach of Nora's light. Far below, a pinpoint of reflected light glistened, but it was too far away for Maddock to accurately judge the distance.

"How deep—" He broke off, realizing that his voice

had been whisper soft, and tried again, with more volume. "How deep are we?"

"About three hundred feet from the entrance." Nora's voice was muffled by her mask. "And the water's surface is another seventy feet down this vertical shaft. We are already deeper than any other tomb in the Valley. It is one reason I believe this was never meant to be a tomb at all."

"What was it then?"

"It is the entrance to a tomb complex, one that thieves would never be able to penetrate. I believe that Sennedjem intentionally carved this shaft deep enough to get below the level of the Nile, and then began a transverse shaft to connect with the river itself."

"That's quite an undertaking."

"Compared to building pyramids?"

Maddock didn't need to see Nora's mouth to know that she was smiling. "Good point."

"Today, the Nile is about three miles away, but the course of rivers changes over time and, before the construction of dams in modern times, the level rose and fell with the seasons. During the annual flood season, the water reached as far as the statues of Amenhotep we saw on the way here. In the dry season, it slowed to a bare trickle. If Sennedjem did most of the original excavation during the dry season, he would not have had to contend with flooded passages. Only as he neared the river bed itself would that become a problem. It is my belief that, while some of his laborers cut the tunnel through the river, others were carving tombs along the way, tombs which could only be reached from that tunnel. Once it reached the Nile and filled with water, there would be no way to enter them."

"At least, not until the invention of SCUBA diving," Bones said.

"It's an interesting theory," Maddock said, "and we should be able to give you a definitive answer. Provided of course the entrance to this hypothetical tomb isn't more than about half-a-mile from where we are."

Nora's eyebrows came together in a look of concern. "Why half-a-mile?"

"Because we only brought a thousand meters of cable for our ROV."

Now the mask did hide Nora's reaction, but Maddock sensed disappointment. After a moment, she shrugged. "Well, let's hope it's enough." She gestured to the pit. "There's not a lot of room to move down there, so you should probably operate from here."

Bones moved to the edge of the pit and after a glance into its depths, nodded in agreement. "Works for me."

He knelt before the Pelican case, opened it to reveal Uma, nestled in a protective layer of egg crate foam. The ROV looked a little like an oversized handheld spotlight mounted on a scaled down set of helicopter landing skids, and indeed, it was equipped with a high-intensity xenon floodlight, but that was only one of its many features. The molded yellow housing concealed small but powerful thruster fans, a high definition video camera with a wide-angle lens, and a small articulated manipulator arm that could grasp small objects for retrieval. A thin cable, sheathed in black insulation, sprouted like a stray hair from the top of the little machine, connecting it to the laptop computer which served as a control interface. Bones drew out several double arm-lengths of the cable, and then held the ROV up with one hand. "Here you go," he said, without looking up.

"Did I miss the part where I lost the coin toss?" Maddock said, jokingly affecting a tone of indignation.

He instantly regretted it.

"Dude, look at those steps," Bones retorted. "You don't seriously expect me to go down there. This is clearly a job for a little guy."

"I'm six inches shorter than you." Maddock held his hands apart to demonstrate the insignificant difference in their respective heights. "Six inches!"

"That's longer than your package." Bones raised a craggy eyebrow, then reached up with his free hand to move Maddock's hands closer together. "There. Six inches." He turned toward Nora, almost certainly grinning behind his mask. "He always exaggerates that."

Even in the relatively dim glow of the flashlight, Maddock could see Nora's furious blush. Hoping to spare the young woman further embarrassment, Maddock took the ROV, cradling it to his chest, and cautiously ventured onto the steps at the edge of the well. "Give me some light," he said.

Almost as soon as he had said it, Uma's xenon spotlight blazed to life. Far brighter than Nora's flashlight, the beam lit up the pit like a small sun. He could see the steps, spiraling down like the grooves inside a rifle barrel, disappearing into the oily blackness at the bottom. The walls of the pit were chalky white near the top, but halfway down, they abruptly transitioned to a velvety black—the mold Nora had warned them about.

As he was about to start down, Nora called out with a final warning. "If you should fall in, whatever you do, don't drink any of the water."

"Always good advice," Maddock replied. "Any particular reason why?"

"Remember how I told you that the water tested as being Nile River water? One of the indicators was the presence of parasites that cause schistosomiasis—what they call 'snail fever.' It's a common disease on the Nile, and the main reason why nobody ever swims in the river."

"So it's not because of crocodiles?" Bones asked.

"No. There aren't any crocodiles north of the Aswan Dam."

"Just parasites," Maddock muttered. "I think I'll just make it a point to stay dry."

As Maddock descended. Bones continued playing out the cable. It trailed out behind Maddock like a lifeline, but he had no illusions about its ability to arrest him should he fall. The cable and the connection to Uma was designed to withstand extreme pressure, not weight. When they operated in deep sea conditions, a secondary wire tether was employed to assist with retrieval, but the limitations of the operating environment, to say nothing of the added bulk of the tether and the winch required to operate it, had prohibited its use here. The thousand yards of interface cable they had brought along was already pushing the limits of practicality.

He found himself unconsciously hugging the wall of the pit as he descended, drawing a measure of comfort from the scrape of stone against his shoulder. That was fine up here where it was dry, but as he approached the horizontal transition line where the black mold had colonized the interior of the well, he had to move more deliberately.

Then, after too many twists to count, he reached the

spot where the steps disappeared into the dark pool. He carefully squatted on the last dry step and eased the ROV out into the water. Despite its not insignificant weight—nearly forty pounds—it did not sink, but instead bobbed on the surface like a toy boat. A gentle push sent it drifting out toward the center of the pit.

"Uma's wet!" His shout reverberated tinnily up the shaft. He didn't know if Bones had heard him, but a few seconds later, a humming sound issued from the little remote submersible. As the interior ballast tanks filled with water, achieving neutral buoyancy, it sank quickly, plunging him once more into darkness.

Resignedly, he dug out his mobile phone and activated the built-in flashlight, then began the long climb back to the top.

He found Bones and Nora huddled over the laptop, following Uma's progress into the well shaft. Nora, her face luminous with excitement, could barely tear her gaze away to acknowledge his return.

"I was right," she said. "Well, right about the transverse shaft."

Maddock knelt behind them and looked over her shoulder. The feed from the video camera showed a rough-hewn keyhole-shaped passage, slick with some kind of organic matter. There were no obvious clues to its dimensions and orientation but the indicators on the edge of the screen showed that the ROV was now moving horizontally along an east-southeast vector.

Toward the Nile.

"The vertical shaft continued another forty feet before intersecting this tunnel," Bones explained. "We're about fifty meters in."

"The passage is large enough for a man to walk

through," Nora said.

"And then some," Bones added. "I think the chica here may be on to something."

Maddock just nodded. It was an encouraging result but wishing wouldn't make it so. Beside them, the interface cable continued spooling out in a slow, mesmerizing rhythm. Despite the constant forward motion, the view on the monitor did not change. The slimy floor, ceiling and walls rolled out to the edges of the screen, but the oblong shadow at the center remained static—an unattainable horizon. Bones called out their progress in fifty-meter increments, and then, as the number edged closer to the final limit, twenty-five. His tone was subdued, anxious.

"Nine hundred," he murmured "Nine twenty-five."

Maddock shook his head, ruefully as Uma reached the end of the line. "Sorry. That's as far as we can go."

Nora's forehead was creased with visible disappointment, but she had not given up hope. "One kilometer. That's not even a quarter of the distance. The entrance to the tomb must be further along." She raised her eyes to him. "What if we extended the cable?"

Maddock shrugged. "It's possible," he equivocated. "We'll have to see what's available locally. If we have to have something shipped here, it will probably be a few days before we can take another crack at it."

"We could dive it," said Bones. The suggestion was offered hesitantly, as if Bones secretly hoped Maddock would immediately veto the idea. It was a measure of the perils of a potential dive that Bones was anything less than gushing with enthusiasm.

"That wouldn't be my first choice," Maddock admitted. "The passage is about forty feet down. The pressure at that depth is about two-and-a-half atmospheres, which means about an hour of air per SCUBA tank. That's probably a bit generous and doesn't allow for much of a safety margin. We have two bottles and I brought along a manifold, so I can rig up a twinset and double that."

"Two hours," Nora said, brightening a little.

He raised his hands in a "hold your horses" gesture. "Slow down. Two hours means one hour out, one hour back. And that may be overly optimistic. We might be able to extend the survey out another mile or so, but that's it. There's no way we're going to be able to explore the whole thing. Not if it really does go all the way to the river."

Nora sagged in defeat.

Normally, Maddock and Bones would have jumped at the chance to go underwater, but this wasn't the open sea, or a cavern full of natural wonders. It was a three-mile long drainage pipe, and Maddock did not relish the idea of spending even one hour in it, much less two.

I guess that's why they call it work, he thought.

"However…" Maddock was grateful for the respirator, which hid his pained grimace. "We did agree to survey this passage for you, and I intend to do just that."

"How?"

"We'll have to rent some additional equipment. A compressor, some spare tanks, maybe a scooter…" He saw her blank look and added, "A diver propulsion vehicle. We'll need it to shuttle the extra tanks into the passage."

"Where will you get this equipment?"

"If I'm not mistaken, there are several dive operators

on the Red Sea coast."

"Yes. In Hurghada and Marsa Alam. But it is a four-hour drive across the desert."

"We can have the dive shop send the equipment by courier. They should be able to have it here by this evening."

She perked up again. "Mr. Fayed might be able to help with that. He has connections with all the tour operators."

Maddock nodded. "Even better." He turned to Bones. "Bring Uma back. We'll head back to Luxor, stash our stuff at the hotel, and then hit up the golden arches for dinner."

"Are you kidding?" Bones said. "I can get that crap anywhere."

Just as Maddock was about to roll his eyes, there was a bright flash in the passage leading back to the surface. His reflexes, honed by military training and real-world experience, kicked in before his brain could even begin to process this new input.

"Get down!" he shouted.

Knowing that Bones would react without hesitation, Maddock wheeled around to Nora, tackling the archaeologist to the floor a fraction of a second before a blast of fire and debris erupted from the passage to engulf them all.

SIX

The cool underground air instantly became blisteringly hot, compressed by the overpressure wave that simultaneously shuddered the ground beneath Maddock, and rocked through him like a gut punch. The larger rocks were like the blows of a sledge hammer, the smaller ones felt like buckshot pellets.

And then, just as quickly as the storm began, it was over.

For several seconds, Maddock lay unmoving, barely aware of Nora shaking under him. He felt like his nerves had gone into overload shut down. A persistent ringing sound filled his head.

He recognized these symptoms for what they were, and more importantly as a sign that he was still alive, but this realization did not automatically translate to hope.

After a few more seconds, he risked opening his eyes.

A mistake. The subterranean gallery had been inundated with a cloud of fine debris that still hung in the air, hiding everything from sight while scouring his eyeballs like a sandstorm. He immediately closed his eyes but the damage was already done. He could feel the grit under his eyelids.

He was vaguely aware of a sound, just below the constant ring. A voice. Nora asking what had happened, or maybe just telling him to get off her. Since his usefulness as a human shield had already ended, he rolled carefully to the side, allowing her unrestricted movement, and as he did, he opened his eyes again but only wide enough to squint through knitted lashes. There wasn't much to see, but after a second or two, his gaze was drawn to a fuzzy yellow glow.

Nora's flashlight.

He crawled over to it and picked it up, then stood. The flashlight's beam swam with dust motes, a solid shaft of light that did little to illuminate the darkness, but when he played it across the floor around him, he could make out Nora, covered in dust and squinting back at him, but otherwise looking no worse for wear. Bones, a few feet away, was just beginning to stir. Through the layer of dust that seemed to coat his entire body, Maddock could see dark splotches—blood seeping from various abrasions and lacerations. Judging by his own condition, Maddock guess none of the injuries would prove life threatening, but that was small comfort. They had a much bigger problem to deal with now.

He shone the light in the direction of the passage leading back to the surface, but instead of the narrow slot through which they had entered, all he saw now was a heap of broken rock spilling. The exit was completely blocked. There was no way of knowing how far up the passage the cave-in extended, but Maddock could tell at a glance that moving the rubble by hand would be impossible.

"What happened?"

The ringing had subsided just enough to let him hear Nora's voice.

"Somebody blasted the entrance," he shouted, uncertain of his own volume.

"Who?"

Maddock had no idea, and answering that question wasn't at the top of his list of priorities. "We'll figure that out once we get out of here."

Bones' deep voice reached out to him. "That was a pretty big freaking charge," he rumbled. His use of the technical term "charge," as opposed to "bomb" was almost certainly deliberately intended to put Nora at ease, if only a little bit, but it didn't lessen the impact of his next pronouncement. "Whoever set it wanted to make sure we wouldn't be leaving through the front door."

"I didn't see another way out," Maddock replied.

Bones cocked his head toward the pit. "There's one way."

"That doesn't go anywhere."

"It goes to the river. We know that much. Nora can wear my mask, and I'll take turns buddy breathing. If I reconfigure Uma for manual operation so we can use her like a scooter, we should have enough air for a one-way trip.

Maddock didn't share Bones confidence in the measures he had just outlined, but there was an even bigger problem with the suggestion. "Just because there's river water down there, doesn't mean we'll find an opening big enough to fit through. The water down there could be filtering in through tons of loose rock."

"Or not," Bones countered. "We know there are tons of rock blocking the way out at this end. I say better to take a chance than sit here and wait to suffocate. Besides, don't you want to know if there really is an undiscovered tomb down there?"

Maddock wanted to argue that they were better off staying put, waiting for someone on the outside to realize what had happened and effect a rescue, but deep down he suspected Bones was right—at least about their chances of making it out through the main entrance. He turned to Nora. "What do you think?"

The archaeologist just stared at him, as if unable to

comprehend the choice he was presenting or the dire reality of their situation, but then she nodded slowly. "I want to know," she said, her voice small behind the dust-clogged respirator. "Before I die."

"Nobody's going to die," Bones asserted.

"Right," Maddock agreed, hoping he sounded as sincere as his friend. "Well, I guess we'd better get started."

While Bones worked on the modifications to Uma, Maddock gave Nora a crash course in SCUBA. Despite Bones' original offer, it was immediately apparent that the full-face masks he and Maddock had brought along were too large for Nora—Bones, thankfully, passed up the opportunity to make an off-color joke—which meant she would be the one buddy breathing from their octopus regulators.

Maddock explained how to equalize the pressure of the descent by popping her ears—a technique called 'the Valsalva Maneuver'—and assured her that all she really needed to do was breathe normally, but he knew that was easier said than done. The weight of water pressing in, combined with the darkness and the close quarters, would quite naturally lead to anxiety, which would in turn cause rapid breathing, and that would quickly exhaust their supply of breathable air. Nora would also be at greater risk for accidental ingestion of the disease causing parasitic flatworms, but the disease was treatable, and besides, it would only be a problem if they actually made it out of the submerged passage. Maddock tried not to think about the unlikelihood of that.

When Bones signaled that he had finished with his preparations, he and Maddock donned their dry-suits, stashing their street clothes and boots in water-proof stuff sacks, along with the dust masks. "We might need them later," he explained, though the paper fibers were already so clogged with dust from the cave-in that their usefulness was almost certainly at an end.

The simple act of dressing down felt to Maddock like a declaration of optimism—a promise to the universe that they would not meet their fate in a submerged tunnel, miles from the surface—but there was also a practical reason for suiting up. The water, while not exactly chilly, would be cold enough to sap their body heat after prolonged exposure. The dry suits would stave off the worst effects, extending their reserves of energy and helping them keep their wits as the journey went on. Nora however, would have no such protection. She would be carried along like so much cargo—cold, wet, and effectively blind as they led her to an uncertain end.

Maddock and Bones both knew what the likely outcome would be, but neither gave voice to their apprehensions. Nor did they waste their breath with platitudes to inspire false hope. Instead, they moved with a sense of urgency, resisting the paralysis of inertia. As soon as they were geared up, they started down the narrow steps into the cylindrical shaft. Bones took the lead, cradling Uma in his arms, while Maddock trailed behind, holding Nora's hand with a determined and insistent grip, compelling her to keep up. When they reached the waterline, Maddock and Bones carefully donned their flippers. Bones then descended the slippery stone steps until he was submerged up to his waist, whereupon he floated Uma, her light blazing, out into the dark water. Only then did he step off, treading water in the middle of the pool.

Maddock gave Nora's hand a squeeze, and said simply, "Our turn." Then, he too ventured down onto into the water, gently pulling Nora in after him.

The young woman shuddered at the first touch of the cool water but to her credit, did not balk. Before stepping off, Maddock held out the octopus regulator and repeated his earlier instructions. "Just breathe normally."

She nodded, shivering as much from apprehension as from the cold, and placed the mouthpiece between her teeth.

With their full-face dive masks and underwater communicators, Maddock and Bones would be able to speak to each other, but there was little to say as they began their vertical journey. Both men held onto Uma, using the submersible's bottom skids as handrails. Bones worked the manual controls, which were housed in a water-tight metal box that dangled like a short tail from the data port, while Maddock continued to hold Nora's hand, signaling her through a prearranged set of gestures and squeezes, to remind her to breathe and Valsalva to equalize the pressure in her inner ear.

By the time they reached the transverse passage, Nora seemed to overcome her initial anxiety, settling into a steady rhythm of breathing, which allowed Maddock to focus on their surroundings, though there wasn't much to see. The passage seemed a lot smaller than it had appeared when viewed remotely, but there was enough room form them to move through. Uma pulled them along at a brisk pace, faster than they would have been able to swim, but Maddock and Bones kicked with their flippers, adding what momentum they could to help overcome the drag of their bodies and hopefully, extend Uma's battery life.

Maddock resisted the urge to compulsively check his pressure gauge every few seconds, choosing instead to monitor their progress with his dive chronometer. There was no way to judge speed or distance, and the passage was so featureless that there was no way to determine when they had passed the furthest point of Uma's first journey.

After thirty minutes had elapsed, he tapped Bones, indicating that it was time to switch places. Only then did Maddock check the pressure gauge. He was dismayed to see that he and Nora had already burned through nearly half his supply of air, but there was nothing to be done about it. It wasn't as if they could take a break from breathing. In another half-hour, they would switch places again, but this time they would only be able to go maybe ten minutes, maybe less, before trading back. And after that?

After that, they would probably drown.

Maddock and Bones both carried pony bottles—small tanks that held a few pounds of air for emergency use—but those would only last a few minutes... A few minutes that they would spend in utter despair.

Maddock shook his head, and focused his attention on the journey, kicking in a steady rhythm and making gentle adjustments to the controls to keep Uma on course. Her batteries would last longer than their air supply. Maybe she would carry their dead bodies all the way to the end of the passage....

Stop it! He chided himself, but his brain refused to let go of the ominous reality of their situation.

Ten minutes ticked by, and ten more. The view ahead, revealed by Uma's blazing xenon light, did not change. But then, just as he was about to signal Bones for another trade-off, he spotted a shadowy gap in the roof of the passage. The mere fact of something different, something to break up the grinding monotony of the journey, infused him with hope. He continued motoring forward until they were under the gap, and then switched off Uma's fans.

It was an opening, big enough for two people to move through abreast. He angled Uma's light up and saw a shaft continued upward at a shallow angle. Even more encouraging, the bottom of this new passage had been cut into stairs, just like those they had descended to reach the unfinished tomb.

"Bones! This is it!" The words felt strange in his mouth. It felt like years had passed since he'd last spoke. "Nora was right. There's another tomb here."

"Well, what are you waiting for?" Bones replied. "We're not getting any younger here."

Maddock suppressed a chuckle, and started purging Uma's ballast tanks as he maneuvered the little ROV into the submerged stairwell. In a few seconds, they were cruising up the passage flying a few inches above the carved steps. "You do realize that this doesn't change our situation a whole lot. This is probably the only entrance."

"Yeah, but just think. Someday, somebody is going to find this place, and when they do, they'll find us in a Pharaoh's tomb. That's way better than drowning in a sewer pipe."

"I'm not really sure how, but…" Maddock trailed off as the light illuminated a shimmering, mirror-like plane cutting across the passage at an angle. Tiny eruptions were bursting across it, air bubbles from their exhalations breaking the surface.

They had made it!

SEVEN

Once they were above the waterline, Maddock removed his mask and took a breath. He had considered continuing to breathe from the SCUBA tanks a little longer, just in case the air was foul, but there seemed little point. The air was musty and tinged with the smell of decay, but seemed otherwise fine, which was a little surprising but welcome nonetheless.

Nora was shivering, her skin pale and clammy, but her eyes were wide in astonishment. "I knew it," she said after spitting out the regulator and working her jaw. "We found it. Akhenaten's tomb. This must be it."

"Well it's something," Bones said. He had Uma tucked under one arm, its light still shining up the shaft. "Do you want the honor of being first in, or should we send Maddock? You know, just in case there are booby traps."

"There aren't any booby traps," she said, though her retort seemed half-hearted.

"Not much of that mold, either," Maddock said, swiping a gloved finger across the wall. The stone around them was stained black as far as they could see, indicating the presence of the same fungus they had seen before, but the accumulation was thin, as if the mold had died off at some point and was only now beginning to colonize again. Something about this nagged at the back of his consciousness.

"Well that's something," Bones said. "I guess we can toss the dust masks."

Maddock shrugged out of his SCUBA rig, unclipped his wet/dry bag, and did exactly that, discarding the stained respirator before delving deeper. He removed a towel which he draped over Nora's shoulders, and then, without asking permission, began rubbing her vigorously to both remove moisture and restore her circulation. After a couple minutes of this, her color returned, after which Maddock and Bones stripped off their dry suits and pulled on their street clothes. Only then did they continue up the steps to see exactly what it was they had found.

The steps continued up another fifty feet before flattening onto a short landing that ended at a pair of doors which appeared to be sheathed in patinaed copper. Nora stepped close and began examining the panels which were adorned with the distinctive iconography of ancient Egypt. Maddock expected her to translate the hieroglyphic writing, but when she finally turned around, her face wore a troubled expression.

"It would seem that Sennedjem's precautions were insufficient to protect the tomb." She pointed to four evenly spaced holes on the door panels—two on each, positioned about where pull handles would have been placed on an ordinary door. "The seal has been removed."

Bones raised a skeptical eyebrow. "You're saying grave robbers made it through that tunnel?"

"I don't know. I just know that the seal that should be right here is gone. Not just broken, but completely removed."

"Maybe the tomb was never used," Maddock suggested. He thought about their discovery of Akhenaten's remains in the secret tomb in the American Southwest. The tomb and its treasures had been brought to the America's by the Spanish centuries after the Egyptian king's death, but it seemed unlikely that his mummy had ever occupied this place. "You said that Tut died before his own tomb was finished. Maybe this project got cancelled at the same time."

Nora shook her head, more a sign of confusion than disagreement, then cautiously inserted her finger into one of the holes.

"Careful," Bones warned, his tone uncharacteristically serious. "Did you check for a curse?"

"There's no curse," she said again, and then without any hesitation, crooked her finger and pulled.

The door swung away easily—too easily for Maddock's liking. He braced himself, half-expecting spikes to shoot out of the walls or something equally terrible, despite Nora's repeated assertions to the contrary, but nothing of the sort happened. Instead, the open door revealed a short passage which opened into a larger room. Even from outside the entrance, Maddock could see large objects inside the room.

"Come on," Nora urged. She grabbed Bones' arm and drew him—and Uma's light—into the passage. Maddock followed, using his phone's light to further illuminate the situation. Here too, a black stain bore witness to the intrusion of mold colonies, but it was faint, as if someone had recently wiped the stone walls clean.

The inner chamber looked more like a storage unit than a treasure vault. Large pieces of furniture, tables, altars, and life-sized statues crowded the space. There was even a fully intact chariot.

"Looks like the tomb robbers missed this place after all," Bones observed.

"I'm not so sure," Nora murmured. "Look at what's not here."

Maddock saw immediately what she was getting at. He recalled Howard Carter's famous comments upon entering the tomb of Tutankhamun: "Everywhere the glint of gold."

There was no gold here.

The objects in the room were made of wood, stone, and fired clay, but there were no precious metals or jewels in evidence. Nor were there any small objects. Everything in the chamber was too big to be easily moved.

Bones picked up on another absent item. "No mummy."

"This is the antechamber," Nora said. "It's kind of the tomb's garage. The mummy will be in a dedicated burial chamber." She motioned to another pair of door panels set against the wall to the right of where they'd entered. "That way."

"Is that where all the treasure will be?" asked Maddock.

"If this tomb follows the standard layout, the most valuable items will be in the canopic chamber, but the only way to get at that is through the burial chamber."

The second set of doors, like the first, were unsealed, a fact that Nora's deep frown said she found disturbing, though she did not say it aloud. She approached the entrance hesitantly, as if afraid of what she might find on the other side.

As before, the door swung open, this time revealing a larger chamber that was considerably less cluttered. In fact, it was almost completely empty, save for a pair of boulder-sized stone sculptures positioned in the center of the room. The exteriors had been chiseled with elaborate patterns, but atop each was the over-sized likeness of a Pharaonic figure lying in repose.

"Sarcophagi," Nora said, breathlessly. She hurried into the room, examining the chests more closely. "Still sealed," she said, with an audible sigh of relief before turning back to her companions. "This is the real treasure."

Maddock nodded. "Any idea who they were?"

She pointed to a line of hieroglyphic symbols carved into the nearest sarcophagus. "This is the cartouche of Neferneferuaten, the predecessor of Tutankhamun."

"You said that's the name Nefertiti used when she ruled as king, right?" he asked.

"That's one popular theory. There are a couple mummies that have been tentatively linked to Nefertiti, but until now, there has never been a sarcophagus positively identified as belonging to Neferneferuaten."

"So if we pop the hood and find out that the dude has lady parts," said Bones, "We'll know for sure."

"Let's say, mostly for sure," Nora amended. "There's another theory that Neferneferuaten might have actually been Meritaten, Nefertiti's daughter.

"Who's in the other one?"

Nora pivoted to examine the cartouche on the seconds sarcophagus. "It's Smenkhkare. After the death of Akhenaten, there were two rulers who held the throne for only a short period of time. Smenkhkare and Neferneferuaten. Not much is known about either one, except that there were tombs prepared for them in Amarna. Because they reigned such a short time—combined, just about three years—before Tutankhamun took the throne, it was always assumed that they were the male alter-egos of Akhenaten's wives or daughters. DNA testing probably won't help much since the family was so completely inbred, but if there are female mummies inside these, then we'll know if that part of the hypothesis is true."

She gestured to indicate the walls of the burial chamber which were covered in rows of hieroglyphs and larger brightly colored painted images of human and divine figures interacting. "These will probably tell the whole story, but it would take me a little time to translate them all."

Bones moved in closer, playing Uma's light over the stone chests. Maddock realized he was recording the discovery. "How do we crack these eggs?"

Nora gaped at him, aghast. "We don't. Not under these conditions."

Maddock decided not to point out that they probably wouldn't get another opportunity, and instead pointed to another set of doors at the far end of the room. "Is that where we should find the canopic chamber?"

"Yes. That's where the richest treasures will be kept, along with the canopic jars containing the vital organs of the entombed mummies."

"Tempting, but I'm still full from the sandwiches," Bones quipped. He finished his visual sweep of the second sarcophagus, and then motioned to the door. "Shall we see what's behind door number three?"

Nora nodded and crossed to the last set of doors, with Bones right behind her, ready to document the big reveal.

"Drum roll, please," he said, and then gave his best attempt at vocalizing the sound. "Badumba-dumba-dumba-dumba."

Nora pulled the doors open, and then let out a gasp

of dismay. Looking over her shoulder, Maddock saw why.

The canopic room was empty.

"No freaking way." Bones shone his light inside. "I guess it's true what they say. You really can't take it with you."

Nora shook her head. "No. Not that." She pointed into the room. "That."

Bones redirected the light and Maddock followed it to another doorway—this one without actual doors—on the wall to their left.

"Door number four," Bones said. "I didn't even know that was an option."

"It isn't. I mean, it shouldn't be. Maybe it leads to another tomb."

Something about the portal struck Maddock as odd, but it took him a few seconds to figure out what it was. "Fresh air," he said. "Do you feel it?"

"You're right," Nora said, her expression brightening hopefully, and then just as quickly falling in disappointment. "That must be a passage back to the surface. I guess that explains what happened to all the treasure."

Maddock's stomach sank. "It's not an undiscovered tomb after all, Somebody else got here first. I'm sorry."

"And recently." She sighed. "But it *is* technically still undiscovered. Unless the looters want to stake a claim."

"I think you're both missing the point," Bones countered, nodding toward the opening. "Can we get the hell out of here?"

Maybe it was the infusion of fresh air, or reordering of priorities, but the significance of the discovery hit Maddock like a slap. "Uh, oh," he muttered. At a quizzical glance from Nora, he went on. "Don't you get it? This is why they tried to kill us."

"They?"

Bones figured it out right away, echoing Maddock's dismay. "Crap. It all makes sense. The guys that tried to rob us at the train station... They were trying to keep us from exploring that passage because they knew we'd eventually find this."

Maddock nodded. "They've probably already moved millions of dollars worth of irreplaceable artifacts onto the black market. If news of this discovery gets out, those pieces may become too hot to handle."

Nora's eyes flashed back and forth between the men, her face moving from confusion to understanding to anger. Then, her eyebrows drew together in consternation. "But... I don't understand. How could anyone have known you were coming?"

"Did you tell anyone else about your discovery?"

"Just Mr. Fayed. And of course, my contact at the Global Heritage Commission."

"Well, somebody spilled the beans," Bones said. "Loose lips sink ships."

"We'll worry about that once we're out of here. My concern now is that they might have figured out that we escaped through the underwater passage. They might be waiting for us outside."

"A very astute observation, Mr. Maddock," intoned a voice from the darkness of the doorway.

A familiar voice.

Maddock tensed, instantly on his guard, but wasn't at all surprised when Nassir Fayed stepped out from the shadows. He wasn't alone. Trailing behind Fayed were four Egyptian men—the same four men that had been waiting in the back-alley garage in Luxor. But this time, they had guns.

EIGHT

Nora gasped. "Mr. Fayed? I don't understand."

Fayed regarded them all coldly for a moment, then turned to one of his henchmen and barked a terse order in Arabic. Since he did not seem inclined to share, Maddock filled the relative silence. "Oh, I think it's all pretty simple. Fayed here decided there was more money to be made selling the treasure than letting you discover it for the Egyptian people."

"Or letting tourists gawk at it," Bones added.

The barbs had their intended effect. Fayed scowled at them. "Tourists," he said, almost spitting out the word.

"Is this true?" Nora asked. "How can you be part of this? You said yourself, these discoveries are the lifeblood of Luxor."

Fayed offered a cruel smile. "Luxor is already dead, my dear. It is a lifeless mummy, decaying little by little. Why should I die with it, when instead, I can be rich?"

"I can think of a few reasons," Maddock said. "For starters, you'll never be able to get away with this. Even if you kill us—and that is what you have planned isn't it?—people know we're here. The Global Heritage Commission knows, and they're going to be wondering what happened to us. They'll find this place, probably a lot sooner than you think, and they'll know that someone raided the tomb. It might take a while, but the trail is going to lead back to you, and when it does, being rich won't help you a bit."

Fayed just laughed. "Very good, Mr. Maddock. You have it all figured out." He looked to his accomplices again, uttering another set of commands in Arabic, then spoke in English. "This way, if you please."

"Not going to kill us here?" Maddock asked.

"Are you in such a hurry to die, Mr. Maddock?"

Bones raised his hand. "I'm not. I'll leave right now."

He took a step toward the exit, which immediately prompted the four gunmen to brandish their weapons. Bones, took a dramatic backward step, and in the process turned so that Uma's light was shining right into Fayed's eyes.

The Egyptian let out a surprised yelp, throwing up a hand to shade his eyes. One of his men advanced on Bones, shouting in Arabic and gesturing with the gun, his meaning easy to understand even if the words were not.

Drop it.

"Okay, okay," Bones said, and then knelt where he stood and began fumbling with Uma's control box.

"Get away from that," Fayed snarled.

"Just trying to save the batteries," Bones explained, unhurriedly.

"I said—"

Uma's light flickered out, plunging the small room into sudden darkness. Fayed's men erupted into angry shouts. Fearing that they might start firing blind, Maddock pivoted into Nora, pulling her down into a protective huddle on the floor, but a moment later, several handheld torches blazed to life, revealing Bones, now standing with his hands raised, with Uma now out of his reach.

"Chill, dudes. No need to freak out."

"That was a very foolish thing to do," Fayed hissed.

Bones affected a look of child-like innocence. "Was it? Sorry."

"I would prefer not to kill you here," Fayed said, "But if you continue to test me…" He let the threat hang in the air, and after a few seconds, took a step back and gestured to the exit. "Move."

Sensing that there was nothing to be gained by further resistance, Maddock nodded to Bones, signaling his intent to go along with their captors, and then did as instructed.

They followed a long, narrow, gently-sloping passage to emerge inside a roofless ruin. After so many hours spent underground, the sunlight was blinding, even inside the four-walled structure, and for a few minutes, all Maddock could do was blink his eyes against the piercing brightness. The world was a blur of sandstone brown and bright blue.

Before his eyes could adjust, Fayed's men led them out of the structure, down a similarly roofless corridor and across a flat sun-scoured area where a white van with dark tinted windows waited. That was about all Maddock could distinguish about the vehicle as he was directed to climb inside. He did, taking a seat in the middle row, scooting across to sit on the far left. Nora sat beside him, and Bones took up the anchor position on the right. Once the doors were closed, he was able to distinguish his surroundings a little better. Fayed had taken the front passenger seat and one of his hirelings was behind the wheel. Another man sat in the open space between them, facing backward to keep an eye— and a gun—on Maddock and the others. The other two men sat in the back row where they also could maintain continuous control over the captives. The van was unremarkable if a little run down, and smelled of stale cigarette smoke and body odor.

Bones wrinkled his nose. "Dude, you guys ever heard of Febreeze?"

None of the men showed the slightest inclination to respond. The driver turned the key and both the engine and the radio began to wail. A few seconds later, they were rolling down a dusty paved road that appeared to follow the course of an ancient wadi.

"That was Deir el-Medina," Nora murmured, evidently recognizing the ruins they had just left behind. "It was the village where the craftsmen who built the tombs resided. We're more than a mile from where we started."

Fayed half-turned to look at them. "Indeed. I honestly didn't expect you to make it out. An impressive feat."

"Gee, thanks," Bones retorted, his tone dripping with sarcasm. "If you want to book us for speaking engagements, we're available, but I'll warn you, we don't come cheap."

Fayed gave a snort of laughter. "Actually, I don't think you are available. I'm afraid you're booked solid for the rest of your life."

"Hey. Leave the jokes to the experts. I'll let you know when we need the douchebag perspective."

"So, what's the plan here?" Maddock said. "Drive us out into the desert, put a bullet in our heads, and let the vultures take care of the evidence?"

Fayed seemed to ponder the question for a moment as if trying to decide whether it was worth the bother of answering, but then he gave an indifferent shrug. "Whatever you may think of me, I'm not a savage. For the time being, you are going to be guests in my home."

"Sweet," Bones said. "Mind if we raid your liquor

cabinet?"

"I don't think they have those here," Maddock said.

Bones affected a look of shock and dismay. "You're kidding. You know, they've got booze at that other Luxor. Just sayin'."

Fayed scowled and turned away, evidently at the limit of his patience. Outside, the van had reached an intersection with a main thoroughfare, and was continuing east. In the near distance, Maddock could see the transition from brown desert to the lush green of the Nile Valley. Almost directly ahead, and rising fast, were the twin sculptures of the Colossi of Memnon. They had come full circle and now appeared to be heading back toward Luxor.

Nora leaned close to Maddock. "He told his men to take us to Gezira el-Tamsah. It means 'crocodile island.'"

"You said there weren't any crocodiles in the river," Bones pointed out.

"There aren't. I mean, not below the dam."

"My home is on Gezira el-Tamsah," Fayed explained without turning to join the conversation. "I own the entire island. The only way to reach it is by boat. And while I do have a few pets, you needn't worry. I'm not going to feed you to them."

Nora went on, speaking only for Maddock's benefit. "He also said they should hold us there until after they released the curse."

"Ha," Bones said. "I knew there was a curse."

"Release the curse," Maddock echoed, fixing Fayed with his stare. The other man continued facing straight ahead.

"That's what he said."

"You don't 'release' a curse," Maddock went on,

mostly thinking out loud. "You release—"

"The kraken!" Bones' boomed dramatically, dropping his already deep voice another octave. "Or the hounds if you're more of a Seinfeld guy."

Nora smiled despite herself.

"Or a bioweapon," Maddock finished. The thing that had been nagging at the back of his mind since emerging from the passage now finally clicked into place. He turned to Nora. "Remember what you said about that black mold being a possible explanation for some of the unexplained deaths attributed to the Curse of the Pharaohs."

She nodded, tentatively. "I said it was one theory."

"I thought it was odd how the walls in the tomb looked like the mold had been cleaned away. Now I understand why. He..." Maddock nodded toward Fayed. "Harvested it."

Her brow furrowed. "Harvested?"

"Collected it. Probably vacuumed it right off the walls so he could cultivate it and harvest the toxin in the spores for use as a weapon. Saddam Hussein did something like that back in the 1990s—weaponized aspergillus mold to produce aflatoxin. Apparently, we interrupted more than just a black-market antiquities racket. Our host is also a terrorist. What's the local flavor down this way? Islamic State? Hezbollah?"

From his oblique angle of observation, Maddock thought he saw a hint of a smile touch Fayed's lips. "It will certainly look that way."

Maddock immediately saw his misstep. "But you're not really a true believer, are you. All you care about is making money."

"How does releasing a biological weapon make him

money?" asked a bewildered Nora.

"It doesn't. He's doing that to divert attention away from the discovery of the tomb. Eventually, somebody else is going to discover that tomb, and figure out that it was only recently looted. When they realize it's also the source of the aflatoxin, they'll assume that the jihadists took the treasure and sold it on the black market. It won't make moving the pieces any easier, but it will deflect attention away from him."

Fayed let out a heavy sigh. "You are very well-informed for a treasure hunter."

Maddock remained impassive, but mentally kicked himself for having overplayed his hand. Fayed probably didn't know that he and Bones were former-SEALs, and that ignorance might just be the one thing that would allow them to escape.

"But killing innocent people?" Nora protested. "How can you do that?"

Fayed ignored the question. The van was now approaching the riverfront. The driver turned off the main boulevard and onto a dirt road that wound through cultivated but otherwise empty fields, eventually reaching a small, private pier where a twenty-four-foot motor launch was moored. The boat, a serviceable Mastercraft Xstar, would have been great as a tow boat for wakeboarding, but Maddock hadn't seen evidence that visitors to Luxor indulged in watersports. It was more likely that this craft was used simply to shuttle back and forth across the river, or presumably, transport the wealthy hotelier to his private island.

Fayed now turned to Maddock. "If you make any attempt to flee or cry out, I will not hesitate to have my men shoot you in the legs, after which, your deaths will be long and painful."

"You win," Maddock said quickly, hoping to keep Bones from making any further displays of bravado.

The doors opened and Fayed's men got out. Although they appeared to be alone and unobserved, the men had put away their guns, but their hands never strayed too far from where they hid under untucked shirttails. One of them, moved close to Nora, gripping her biceps and roughly putting some distance between her and the others; the clear implication that her safety would depend on Maddock and Bones behaving themselves. Another gestured to the boat and barked something in Arabic.

Maddock complied, heading down the dock to climb into the waiting craft. As Bones clambered over the gunwale to take a seat beside him, Maddock realized that Fayed had remained at the van, along with the driver.

"Guess he's got somewhere else to be," Bones muttered.

"You think maybe he's going to launch the bioweapon attack right now?"

"Maybe we screwed up his timetable by surviving longer than planned."

"Or just by showing up at all. I think his original plan was just to derail us by stealing Uma. When that didn't work, he had to take things up a notch. I've got a feeling he's making this up as he goes." Maddock stopped talking as the remaining gunmen escorted Nora to the boat and boarded.

While the Mastercraft could theoretically seat up to fourteen people, it felt overcrowded with just six— probably because, save for Nora, they were all physically imposing figures. The boat sank a little lower in the water with each addition. Fayed's men however seemed to know what they were doing. One of them loosened the moorings and then took a seat at the wheel, while the other two positioned themselves facing the captives, their guns out again, but held low and concealed from casual view.

The inboard roared to life, and the boat backed away from the dock. When it was floating clear, the pilot pointed the prow south, and gradually increased throttle until the boat was skipping across the wakes that crisscrossed the river.

"Think these guys speak English?" Maddock asked. He had to almost shout to be heard over the roar of the motor, and one of their captors shot him a warning glance.

"Dunno," Bones said, and then looking the wary gunman in the eye said, "My friend is interested in camel humps." He winked suggestively. "You guys are into that, right?"

Nora grimaced apprehensively, but the man's glower remained about the same. His eyes darted back and forth from Maddock to Bones, clearly expecting them to try something, but the insult seemed to have gone entirely over his head.

Bones looked back over at Maddock. "*No habla.* I guess you've got a plan?"

"Working on it," Maddock said. "Nora, you can swim, right?"

"Yes," came the tentative reply, and then. "Oh, you don't mean…" She glanced at the gunmen, and then mouthed the word, "Jump?"

Maddock guessed they were traveling at about thirty miles an hour. Exiting at that speed would be unpleasant, but not as unpleasant as getting shot, which was in fact his greater concern. Even if the three of them all managed to leap out into the river—and survive the impact—their captors would only need to cut speed, come about, and either pick them off one by one, or simply run them down. No, if they were going to get out of this, they would have to do more than just jump.

As Maddock considered and rejected various strategies for overpowering the men, the boat continued on its upriver journey. They briefly had an unrestricted view of the sprawling Karnak Temple Complex on the east bank of the river, but were soon all but surrounded by ferries, feluccas and other craft roaming the waterway. Fayed's men remained especially alert whenever they passed close to another vessel, but as the left the more densely populated urban center behind, transitioning into the fertile agricultural zone, the men seemed to relax a little. Maddock got the sense that they were nearing their destination; if he didn't do something and quick, the chance might be lost.

He caught Bones' eyes and gave a slight nod—the signal to be ready—and then slowly, carefully, stood up.

The gunmen reacted instantly, brandishing their weapons, thrusting them at Maddock and shouting incomprehensible commands.

Which was pretty much exactly what he had hoped they would do.

Maddock raised his hands quickly in a show of harmlessness. "Hey, it's okay." He called out. "No problem here. Just stretching my legs." And then, in the same tone, without missing a beat, he added. "Now would be a really good time."

With their attention laser-focused on Maddock, the

gunmen were half-a-second slow in noticing that Bones was also on his feet and, unlike Maddock, moving. Before they could adjust their aim, he darted toward the control console and, leaning over the surprised helmsman, shoved the throttle all the way forward.

NINE

Maddock had not known precisely how Bones would seize on the opportunity, but he trusted his friend to make it something dramatic, and knew that he would have to react quickly to protect himself and Nora from whatever followed. Even as the attention of the two gunmen shifted toward Bones, Maddock spun around and threw himself onto the still seated Nora, covering her with his body and wrapping his arms around her. His thinly-sketched plan had been to scoop her up and leap from the fast-moving speed boat into the river, but the last part proved unnecessary.

As the screws suddenly revved to full throttle, the front end of the boat rose high in the air, like a motorcycle popping a wheelie. The abrupt shift had the effect of catapulting the boat's occupants, launching them backward, even as the boat rose out of the water like a kite attempting liftoff.

Maddock, still embracing Nora, curled himself into a protective ball and braced for impact as the world around him spun crazily. When it finally came, the splashdown was less of a jolt than expected. The surface, already churned up by the boat's passage, acted like an air cushion, softening the blow. As the frothing wake enveloped him, he caught a fleeting glimpse of the boat, teetering on its stern, and slowly heeling over.

He relaxed his hold on Nora, but maintained a grip on her arm so they would not be separated, and then immediately began kicking back toward the surface. When he popped up a moment later, he spotted the boat, upside down, just a few yards away. One of the gunmen was thrashing in the water nearby, his hands empty, his weapon presumably now settling into the mud at the river's bottom. Nora was treading water beside him, a little dazed, but apparently unhurt. There was no sign of Bones, but Maddock did not doubt that his friend, the only one of the boat's occupants who had known what was about to happen, had bailed out and was even now, striking out for dry ground.

The closest land, was about a hundred yards away, on the west bank. Maddock pointed toward it, and shouted, "There!" Then, with one hand still in contact with Nora, he leaned into the water and started swimming furiously.

Once they were moving, Nora rallied and was soon swimming unaided. The approaching island seemed to energize her for a final push, and as their strokes brought them into the reeds lining the shore, she got her feet under her and half-ran, half-splashed through the muddy shallows. Maddock lingered a moment longer in the concealment afforded by the marsh, checking behind them to verify that Fayed's men had not somehow gotten ahead of them to lay in ambush. He didn't see the gunmen, but he did spot Bones, only about twenty yards away, likewise crawling through the grass.

As he rose to his feet, he turned and looked out across the water. The capsized boat was drifting with the current, two bedraggled figures clinging to its upturned hull. A moment later, Maddock spotted the third man, thrashing ineffectually in an attempt to reach his comrades.

Maddock breathed a sigh of relief and turned to Bones. "So that was your plan?"

"Pretty much," Bones replied, grinning. "Hey, it worked, right?"

"I guess it did at that." Maddock turned to take in their new surroundings, a gentle slope rising from the river, covered in a lush carpet of river grass and large-leafed palms that fully blocked their view of what lay to the west. "Any idea where we are?" he asked Nora.

She nodded. "This is Gezira el-Mozh. Banana Island. The only way to come or go is by boat. I'm afraid there's not much here."

Bones snorted. "You're kidding. Leave it to Maddock to get us all stranded on a tropical island in the middle of the desert."

"Me?" Maddock protested. "You're the one who capsized the boat, Gilligan."

"Oh, yeah? Well why don't you figure out a way to get us out of here, Professor? Wait, having Professor here would actually be a good thing." Pete Chapman, nicknamed "Professor," was another of their old SEAL comrades, known for his nimble mind and breadth of knowledge.

Maddock quirked an eyebrow at his friend, then turned back to Nora. "When you say 'not much here…'?"

"It's a sort of nature preserve. Tourists sometimes come here to walk and pick bananas. There's a small café and a menagerie. Just a few animals in cages."

"You said the only way here is by boat. Is there a regular ferry service?"

"Not that I'm aware of. Most people come over by felucca."

"Let's get to the dock. Maybe we can find someone to give us a ride." He searched the trees until he spotted what looked like a clearing, and started for it.

"Shouldn't we just call the police?" Nora said. "Let

them know what Fayed is up to."

"A couple of foreigners accusing an upstanding local businessman of grave robbing and terrorism," Bones countered. "I'm sure they'll jump right on that."

"I think we might be the only ones who can stop him," said Maddock.

"But we don't even know what his plan is."

"We'll figure that out on the way." He reached the clearing and saw that it was actually a path leading between the rows of banana trees. To his right, he had an unrestricted view going all the way to the north tip of the island, and there, bobbing in the water just off shore, was a small sailboat with a triangular sail—a felucca. "That should do the trick," he said, and then broke into a run.

They emerged from the path near a grassy area dotted with café tables. A few of the tables were occupied by sunburned tourists who goggled in disbelief at the bedraggled trio. Maddock paid no heed but continued past toward the water's edge where several sailboats had been run up onto the shore. He didn't see any crewman, which he decided was probably a good thing—they didn't have time to explain their needs, nor the resources to make an offer that a poor Egyptian sailor would be unable to refuse. That left only one real option.

"That one," he called out, pointing toward an open, broad-beamed sailboat that was barely longer than the speedboat, and about half the length of the largest boat in the line. This was one instance where bigger definitely wasn't better. As he reached the boat, he threw his shoulder against the prow, shoving it back out into the water, even as he shouted, "All aboard."

Beside him, Nora let out a gasp of disbelief. "Wait. We're stealing it?"

"Borrowing," Bones replied. "I don't think it will fit into our checked luggage when we fly home. Especially not with all of Maddock's beauty products." He then scooped her up in his arms and splashed out into the river, running alongside the craft until he was able to deposit her into its open cockpit, whereupon he immediately clambered aboard. Maddock, knowing that they would need all the momentum he could muster, kept pushing even after the boat was floating free. When he was waist deep in the river, he gave it one final shove and then threw himself flat in the water, swimming out to catch the drifting boat.

A moment later, he heaved himself up onto the gunwale, and with an assist from Nora, managed to climb inside. Bones was already pulling on the line to raise the enormous offset triangle that was the felucca's signature lateen sail, so Maddock crawled back to the rudder and, turned the boat toward the middle of the river, letting the current carry them away. Behind them, a small crowd was gathering on the shore, hurling angry shouts that carried across the water, but apparently none of them were willing to swim out after the stolen craft.

"So, you guys are pirates, too?" Nora remarked.

"We are now." Maddock gave a half-hearted laugh, although he couldn't tell if she meant it as a joke. Before he could answer, the sail gave an audible pop as it filled with wind. There was only a light breeze, blowing from the north against the current, but Bones, deftly maneuvered the boom, angling the sail into the wind, while Maddock used the rudder to steer toward the East Bank, tacking against the wind to keep them moving with the current, toward downtown Luxor.

As Banana Island receded into the distance, Nora

came back to join him. "You do realize that the people back there have probably already called the police," she said, and this time, there was no mistaking her tone as humorous. "Which is what we should have done in the first place."

"Well, at least this way, we'll get their attention," Maddock replied. "But until that happens, we've got to focus on stopping Fayed."

"And how are you going to do that? We don't even know exactly what his plan is."

Maddock couldn't argue that point. "You said he owns a resort."

She nodded. "The Jawahrat al-Nayl." She turned, scanning the East Bank downriver of their position, and then pointed. "It's there."

Maddock couldn't tell which of the enormous multi-storied buildings she was looking at, but the general area was only about half-a-mile away. They would be there in just a few minutes. "Maybe somebody there will be able to tell us where he is."

As the resort loomed closer, Bones turned the sail into the wind, slowing their approach while Maddock maneuvered the boat alongside the pier. He half expected to find a line of city police officers waiting to arrest them for hijacking the felucca, but it seemed to be business as usual on the riverfront.

"Nice place," Bones said, approvingly, as they entered the lavishly appointed lobby, which appeared to have been modeled after a Sultan's palace. After so much time spent in the desert heat, the air conditioning was a welcome relief, if a little chilly. "This is where we were supposed to spend the night, isn't it? You think they kept our reservation?"

"Can't hurt to ask," Maddock said, and veered toward the reception desk.

A long-polished wood counter separated the hotel's employees—all of whom were male and attired in immaculate Navy-blue business suits—from the guest area. On the wall behind the men were large framed posters of happy people enjoying the various activities available to hotel residents—desert safaris, hot air balloon rides, excursions to the Red Sea shore for SCUBA diving and snorkeling—each bearing the legend in bold exciting script: "Book your adventure today!"

One of the men, noticing their approach cast a disdainful eye at Nora. Maddock stepped in front of her, commanding the man's attention as he closed the remaining distance. He leaned over the counter, palms placed flat on the surface, and in his best, command voice, barked, "We're here to meet with Nassir Fayed."

The man snapped to attention at the mere mention of the name, but he quickly regained his supercilious demeanor. "And who are you?"

His English was as impeccable as his suit.

Bones now joined Maddock at the counter, leaning over it and towering above the clerk. "We're from the Tourism Board. We've had several complaint of bedbugs at this establishement." He spoke loud enough for everyone in the lobby to hear. "Nasty little bloodsuckers. We've received some disturbing reports, so we'll need to conduct a snap inspection of your hotel. Every room. Shouldn't take more than a couple days, but you'll need to move your guests somewhere else until we're done." He paused a beat, and then added in a low, conspiratorial tone, "Unless of course, Mr. Fayed can convince us that there really isn't a problem."

Maddock stifled a laugh as the man's expression changed again. He recoiled a step, and then glanced nervously in the direction of his co-workers, all whom now seemed intensely interested in looking at their computer monitors. "I… Ah, let me get the maître d'."

"You do that," Maddock said.

As the man scurried away, exiting through a door behind the counter, Bones leaned close. "This is a waste of time. These guys won't be in the loop."

"I know," Maddock replied, already having reached the same conclusion. He stared at the back wall, an idea starting to form. "What's the most effective way to disperse the mold spores? I mean for targeted effect."

Bones emitted a thoughtful rumble. "He probably doesn't have access to artillery shells. A bomb would just destroy the toxins. Maybe he's just going to drive around and fling buckets of the crap out the window?"

"I think he's a little smarter than that," Maddock replied, still staring straight ahead. A moment later, the clerk emerged from the back office, accompanied by another man, this one wearing a black tuxedo. Both moved quickly to the counter, the man in the tuxedo already raising his hands in a placating gesture. Maddock cut him off with a wave.

"We changed our minds," he said. "We can do this tomorrow. Right now, I think I'd like to see about booking a balloon ride."

TEN

"The balloons only fly very early in the morning, when the air is cool," explained the maître d'hôtel, clearly confused by this abrupt shift. "I can book you for a flight tomorrow. Or perhaps some other activity? You may stay here, with our compliments, of course."

"And get eaten alive by bedbugs?" Bones snapped. "I don't think so."

"I'd really like a balloon ride," Maddock insisted. "Where do they take off?"

"The staging area is on the West Bank."

"It's near the Temple of Hatshepsut," Nora supplied.

Maddock scowled. "What's the fastest way there?" He didn't wait for an answer. "No, scratch that. I want you—" He stabbed a forefinger at the man's chest. "—to take us there. Right now."

The man goggled at him for a moment, but then gave an obsequious nod. "Of course."

He ducked back through the door, then emerged a moment later from another door that opened into the lobby. "Please, follow me."

As they headed back toward the riverside entrance, Bones leaned in again. "Balloon ride?"

"It's the perfect delivery platform. He can fly over all the major tourist hot spots and disperse the stuff into the air. I doubt anyone on the ground would even notice. They'd chalk it up to blowing dust. The effect probably wouldn't even be felt for hours, maybe even days."

"Okay, as crazy ideas go, it's not the worst one you've had."

Maddock turned to Nora. "We can handle this from here. You should probably find somewhere safe to hole up. Contact the authorities. Maybe Dr. Zahi can help."

"And who will translate for you?" She shook her head. "No. I'm staying with you."

Maddock wasn't inclined to argue with the young woman. She certainly wasn't wrong about the language barrier, and after everything they had survived together, he would have been surprised if she had taken him up on the offer to bow out.

The maître d' led them out onto the boardwalk, back down to the pier and right past their "borrowed" felucca. Maddock could hear the wail of sirens in the distance and wondered if it was the police, heading to investigate reports of the stolen sailboat tied up at the resort's dock, or responding to some other completely unrelated crisis. He hoped it was the former, and that upon arrival, the police would learn that the "pirates" had left with the maître d', heading to the balloon staging area on the West Bank. If they were going to stop Fayed, they would need some support from the authorities, but they would have to catch him red-handed, in the act of launching a bio-terror attack.

He didn't allow himself to dwell on all the ways this might go wrong.

The hotel manager ushered them onto a medium-sized pontoon boat, similar to the party barges used by fishing charter companies, and in no time at all, they were once again motoring across the Nile, this time heading north, downriver.

The journey took all of five minutes, and when they tied up on the far shore, the maître d' hastened out ahead of them, negotiating with one of the waiting taxi drivers to take them the rest of the way. Maddock, Bones and Nora piled into the back seat of the cab, and then they were off again, traveling back toward Deir al-Bahari.

Whether it was the fact that the route had become so familiar, or the skill of the driver, the journey seemed to take no time at all. After passing the Colossi of Memnon yet again, they turned north along the desert road, but as they made the hard-left turn leading back to the Mortuary Temple of Hatshepsut, Maddock realized their destination was actually much closer. Less that a quarter of a mile further up the road, two large, bright red, bulb-shaped objects protruded from the desert floor—a pair of hot-air balloons, fully inflated and evidently ready for take-off.

"Crap," Bones muttered. "I hate it when you're right."

Maddock clapped a hand against the back of the driver's seat and pointed at the rising balloons. "There. You've got to get us there. Right now."

But even as the taxi's engine revved, the little car veering off the paved road onto the primitive track that led to the staging area, Maddock could see that they were too late. Jets of orange flame were shooting up from the burner units atop the gondolas, heating the air inside the balloon envelopes, and already, the balloons were beginning to rise. One of the balloons was more than a hundred yards away, the bottom of its wicker gondola at least twenty feet above the ground, but the other one— half as far away—had just broken contact with the earth.

"That one," Maddock shouted, pointing again. "Head for that one. Ram it!"

The driver complied, but in the three seconds it took for them to cross the distance, the gondola lofted into the air. The cab driver, hesitating at the last instant, applied the brakes as the over-sized basket filled the windshield, skidding to a stop almost directly under it.

Bones threw open his door and made a desperate leap, launching from the door frame. His long arms gave him enough reach to snare one of the rope loops that dangled like handles from the base of the gondola, but the addition of his weight did nothing to slow the aircraft's rise. Instead, he too began rising with it.

Maddock threw himself across the back seat, snagging Bones' booted foot a fraction of a second before it disappeared above the roof of the taxi, but even this did little to arrest the balloon's rise. The simple aircraft could easily bear twenty passengers aloft, and from what he had glimpsed on their approach, they were well below capacity.

As he too was drawn up and out of the vehicle, Maddock hooked one arm around the doorpost, and anchored himself. The strain was beyond anything he had expected, a titanic tug-of-war, with Bones acting as the rope. It was a battle he didn't think he could win, but if he let go, Bones would be taken up and, when the big man's grip eventually failed, he would plummet to his death. Maddock wasn't going to let that happen.

With a heave, he pulled Bones back down. Six inches. A foot. Two.

Bones, uttering a howl that Maddock momentarily mistook for pain, also started pulling, flexing his arms and dragging the gondola lower still. The superhuman effort brought him down far enough that his legs were once more inside the interior of the taxi, and he twisted around wedging his free foot under the hinge of the open door.

"I got this," Bones rasped. "Do something else."

Maddock knew what "something else" meant. He

released Bones' foot and squirmed out past him, belly-flopping onto the gritty desert floor, but immediately sprang to his feet and looked up at the gondola, now floating just a couple feet above his head. Without a moment's hesitation, he scrambled onto the taxi's rear end and then up onto its roof. There was an ominous popping sound as the roof panel dimpled under his weight, but he ignored it, flexing his knees and swinging his arms back for added momentum. Then, he jumped.

His reaching hands caught the lip of the gondola basket, and this time, the sudden addition of his mass caused the whole affair to wobble a little. He got his knees up, the toes of his boots clawing against the basket weave for purchase, and managed to heave himself up and onto the padded rim of the gondola.

In that instant, he got his first real look at the balloon's occupants, two Egyptian men, one of whom he recognized despite the white respirator covering the lower half of his face. Fayed's driver. There was no sign of Fayed himself—he was either in the other balloon, or overseeing the operation from the ground—but if the man and his protective dust mask wasn't confirmation enough that they had been right about Fayed's plan, the two thirty-gallon clear plastic bags filled with something that looked like black dust established it beyond any doubt.

The two men gaped at him in disbelief for a moment, but as Maddock rolled over into the gondola, they shook off their paralysis, and started toward him.

Maddock landed in a crouch, the basket wobbling a little under him like the deck of a boat at sea. He stayed low, but charged the nearest man, driving his shoulder into the man's gut and knocking him backward, but even as he made contact, he felt grasping hands close on his own shoulders, spinning him around and slamming him into the side of the gondola. There was a sickening crunch—not his bones breaking, but strands of woven wicker, splintering under the impact. Fayed's goon loomed over him, his right arm drawing back to deliver a knockout punch. Maddock didn't try to block the incoming blow, but instead dropped heavily onto the floor of the gondola, ducking under the swing, and counter-attacked with a kick that drove up into the man's abdomen. The force of the blow launched the man into the air just as the swaying gondola dipped behind him. He hit the edge of the basket, flipped over the side and vanished from sight, but a half-second later, Maddock heard the resounding thud of a body hitting something solid.

The struggle had set the gondola pitching back and forth like an old rope swing, and Maddock was afraid that if he tried to get his feet under him, he too might go over. His remaining foe likewise made no attempt to rise; he didn't need to. Still sitting with his back to the far end of the gondola, the man slowly, carefully reached under his shirt and drew out a pistol.

For a fraction of a second, Maddock considered trying to charge the man, but with the platform heaving under him, he figured he had a less than fifty-fifty chance of surviving the attack. But as he measured the distance, his gaze settled once more on the plastic bags full of mold spores. One of them was within easy reach, and in a flash of inspiration—or more likely desperation—he snatched it to him and held it over his head with both hands as if it was a rock which he intended to hurl at the man. "Don't do it," he warned.

Even though the man's respirator probably would have protected him from exposure, the threat caused him to hesitate, but only for a second or two. Then, the gun resumed its slow rise, the gaping hole of the muzzle wavering back and forth as he tried to aim. Maddock's feint had only delayed the inevitable.

But that delay made all the difference.

Before the man could fire, Maddock glimpsed movement to his left. Someone—Nora!—had appeared just outside of the gondola.

How...?

The gunman noticed her as well, and almost reflexively shifted his weapon toward her.

Maddock threw the bag in the direction of the man's face, and in the same motion, launched himself across the gondola. As he moved, Maddock drew in a quick breath, just in case the bag ruptured, but it proved to be an unnecessary precaution. Its loosely-packed contents were so light, it seemed to drift, rather than fly across the intervening space, but it's bulk hid both Maddock and Nora from the gunman's view just long enough for Maddock to cross the gondola and get inside the man's reach. A knife-hand blow to the wrist knocked the gun away, sending it spinning out away from the gondola, and as the unbroken bag tumbled to the deck, Maddock delivered a second punch that connected squarely with the man's chin, putting him down for the count.

Maddock whirled to check on Nora. It took him a moment longer to realize that the balloon—without the constant flame from its jet-engine like burners—had sunk back down, the gondola now almost at ground level.

Bones appeared beside her, his hands gripping the

lip of the basket, still anchoring the balloon though with considerably less effort than before. His gaze settled on the garbage bags, and he frowned. "Well, that takes care of this one, but I think Fayed's in that one." He thrust his chin over his shoulder toward the second balloon, which was not only continuing to rise, but drifting in a southeasterly direction, carried by the breeze.

The partial victory stung almost as much as outright defeat, but as he stared at the retreating balloon, Maddock's frustration transformed first into rage, and then, resolve. "Climb in," he said in a low voice that was almost a growl. "We're going after him."

ELEVEN

Bones, seemingly anticipating Maddock's decision, was already hoisting himself up onto the padded edge. Nora however goggled at him a moment longer. "So now we're air pirates," she remarked, though this time with a hint of a smirk. "Do you actually know what you're doing?"

"Don't worry," Bones said, extending a hand to assist her with boarding. "This isn't our first balloon-jacking."

"You're kidding." She shook her head. "No, somehow I don't think you are."

"I guess technically we didn't jack the thing, since we weren't actually in it at the time. We just sort of let it go." He nodded toward Maddock. "It was his idea."

"We've led interesting lives." Maddock had already turned away, moving to the center of the gondola where an upraised platform held the burner unit high overhead. A single pull-handle hung down from it, and when he gave it an experimental tug, a quasi-Biblical pillar of fire blossomed into existence above them, shooting up through the flame-retardant Nomex skirt around the opening of the balloon, and high up into the nylon canopy. There was another handle, this one connected to a line that snaked up into the vast envelope above. Maddock guessed it was some kind of vent control for rapid descent but decided not to mess with it.

"Seems simple enough," he said, and then glanced over at the still unconscious gunman. "Maybe lighten our load a little?"

Bones grinned and with a deft move, scooped the man up and heaved him unceremoniously over the side.

Maddock pulled the handle again, this time holding it down for a sustained blast. The noise was deafening, and the radiant heat was barely endurable, so after counting to five, he let off, but only for another five second interval. He kept this cycle—five on, five off—and on the third iteration, the balloon began to loft skyward again. Maddock could feel the wind—a gentle breeze, maybe only five miles per hour—pushing the balloon along in the same direction as its twin. That was small comfort. The other balloon had shrunk to the point where Maddock could cover it with an outstretched thumb, and while it was no longer pulling away, they weren't getting any closer, either.

Like the felucca, the balloon relied completely on wind for motive force, but unlike the sailboat, there was no way to maximize the push, much less steer. The choices available to balloonist were up and down. Because the atmosphere wasn't a uniform, homogeneous bubble of air, but a swirling mass of air currents of different speed and temperature interacting in three-dimensions, it was possible to steer, after a fashion, by rising or falling into a breeze blowing the desired direction, but there was no way to make the balloon go faster.

Maddock pulled the handle again, this time counting to ten before releasing it. He guessed they were at least a hundred feet up, rising about five feet per second.

Bones joined him. "So are we just going to enjoy the view, or do you have some kind of cunning plan?"

"You mean beyond hoping that the wind changes and blows him back our way?" Maddock sighed. "Not really."

"Even if the wind does change, it won't help," Nora pointed out. "It would blow us away from him."

"And then there's the problem of what to do if, by

some miracle, we do catch him," Bones went on. "It's not like we can force him down. Even if we got that close, we'd just bump together like a couple of fat asses at a buffet."

Maddock almost laughed at the image, but it gave him an idea. "Only if we bump side-to-side. What if we tried to 'sit' on him?" He indicated the second, as yet untouched handle. "Get above him, and then pull the release vent."

Bones eyebrows came together in a look of consternation. "I'm not sure it works like that."

Maddock knew his friend was probably right, but absent any other plan, he activated the burner for another ten-count, lifting the balloon even higher. They came level with the other balloon, which looked about as big as a standard light bulb held at arm's length, and then rose even higher, so that they were looking down at it. Far below and directly ahead, not even a mile away, was a sprawling rectangle on the desert floor, studded with multiple sand-colored protrusions—the ruins of some massive temple complex. They were still too far away to make out any people moving in the ruin but arrayed at one edge of the complex were more than a dozen waiting tour buses.

"That's the Ramesseum," Nora said. "The mortuary temple of Ramesses II."

"Think that's his target?"

Nora frowned uncertainly. "It's not the most popular site, but it is on most of the tour routes."

"Beggars can't be choosers," Maddock said. "He can't fly around up here all day hoping the wind takes him to a better target. He's going to dump the stuff there. I can feel it."

As if to confirm his gut instinct, the other balloon began descending, venting hot air to get closer to the ruins of the Ramesseum. Maddock turned to grip the vent handle, intending to pull it and follow the other balloon down but stopped short when he realized that, not only was the other balloon descending, it was also getting closer. The pilot—presumably Fayed—had lost the wind and was now merely drifting toward the ruin, while Maddock and the others were still moving with the breeze.

"Sit on him," Maddock repeated, grinning. He gave the burner another five-second blast to maintain their current altitude, and then shouted. "Bones, tell me when we're directly over him."

Bones shook his head, then turned to Nora. "I can't reason with him when he gets like this. Better hold on to something."

Nora gaped in disbelief for a moment but then complied without comment.

Maddock ignored both of them, watching intently as Fayed's balloon approached and then, at least from his perspective, appeared to dip below the edge of the basket. "Say when," he urged.

Bones was silent for several seconds, then shook his head again. "It's no good. We're gonna miss him."

Maddock hasted to join Bones at the edge, and saw that his friend wasn't wrong. The second balloon was a big red dot below them, maybe two or three hundred feet down, and less than a hundred above the ground, but it wasn't directly below them, and as he watched, Maddock saw that dot rolling along almost perfectly parallel to the rim of their gondola. Although it was impossible to judge distances, Maddock knew that it was probably a lot further away than it looked, but refusing to accept defeat, he swiveled back to the vent control and pulled hard.

The balloon did not exactly plummet from the sky. For a few seconds, Maddock wasn't even sure anything was happening; had be been wrong about the purpose of the handle? But then Bones called out again, his tone verging on frantic. "Crap! Up! Up!"

Maddock immediately released the handle, and gave the burner another blast which he held until Bones sagged back in visible relief. "Better."

Maddock rejoined him at the side of the gondola and saw that Bones' panic was well-founded. The ground had come up a lot faster than he'd realized. Another second or two of venting, and they might have slammed into the desert floor like a meteor.

The red dot of the other balloon had swelled to the size of a small planet, its top maybe fifty feet below the bottom of their gondola, and at least as far away.

Maddock rapped his knuckles against the edge of the gondola. "Damn it. So close."

"Not close enough," Bones countered. "Maybe if we all blow really hard, we can get closer."

Maddock stared at the other aircraft and the turned back to the interior of the gondola. "Is there something we can throw at him?"

"How about our shoes," Nora suggested.

Maddock didn't know if she was being serious or sarcastic. In the Arab world, throwing shoes at someone was a major league insult, but that was about all they had left.

Fayed had beaten them. He was just seconds away from the edge of the temple complex, seconds away from unleashing his "Pharaoh's Curse" onto a crowd of unsuspecting innocents and there was nothing they could do to stop him.

Maddock pounded his fist on the edge of the gondola in frustration, wishing he could hurl himself across the void….

He jolted as if he had received an electric shock.

No, that's insane, he told himself, and then, *Why not?*

He spun back to the center and initiated another burn. When he was certain that the balloon was rising again, he let go and headed back to the edge. The balloon was starting to drift again, pushed by the winds aloft but was still about the same lateral distance from Fayed's balloon, though now at least a hundred feet above it.

His brain automatically started calculating angles and glide vectors… And the odds of surviving what he intended.

Don't think about it. Just do it.

He grasped one of the upright supports and pulled himself up onto the rim of the basket, balancing precariously on the edge.

Bones looked up at him. "Uh, dude? Please, tell me you're not thinking of doing something batsh—"

Maddock didn't hear the rest. He had already jumped.

TWELVE

Fayed could not believe they were still alive. Maddock, Bonebrake, and that damned Majdy woman. They were thorns in his side, the mere thought of them causing his anger to boil. Sweat rolled down his neck. Not even the breeze as they flew along could cool the heat rising inside of him. They were so close to their target!

"I'll give them full marks for persistence," Gamal said, looking up at the balloon that pursued them.

"They do seem to have a knack for escaping," Fayed admitted. Stilling himself to calm, he watched as the other balloon continued to rise. He wanted to lash out, to break something, hurt someone. But it would not do to lose control in front of his underlings. He could not help but feel a grudging respect for Maddock and Bonebrake. What were the odds that, in addition to being archaeologists, divers, and military-trained, the men also knew how to pilot a balloon?

"They escaped us in the city. They survived the blast at the well. Then they escaped the boat and now they're pursuing us? Who are they, anyway?" A slight note of reverence tinged Gamal's voice.

Fayed shook his head. "They are people who shall soon be dead. That is all that matters."

"What if they catch us?"

Fayed whipped his head around, ready to berate his underling, but he realized there was no fear in Gamal's eyes, no trepidation in his voice. It was a strategic question.

"What are they going to do if they manage to get close to us? A hot air balloon version of kite fighting?" He forced a cold smile. "But as long as we focus on keeping ahead of them…" He cut off at the expression on Gamal's face. Wide-eyed, he pointed at Maddock's balloon.

"What is he doing?"

In their many years of working together, Bones had witnessed Maddock take some pretty crazy chances. He'd taken his share of them as well—several in the last few hours, actually. But jumping out of a hot-air balloon without a parachute? That was in a class by itself.

Yet, as he watched Maddock leap into the air, arch his body like a high-diver, and then flatten out, head tilted down, arms swept back, legs extended, turning his body into a living wing, Bones realized that his friend knew exactly what he was doing. Maddock's glide was a thing of beauty—not quite flying, but as close to it as a person could get without a wingsuit. His glide ratio was less than 1:1, meaning he was moving vertically faster than he was moving forward, but he *was* moving forward, falling in a parabolic curve that would, just barely, bring him into direct contact with Fayed's balloon.

Then, it was over. Maddock arrowed into the curved side of the other balloon, and vanished as the red nylon envelope enfolded him, swallowing him from Bones' view. The balloon had acted like a high-fall stunt airbag, which had no doubt been Maddock's thinking prior to making his leap of faith. The force of the collision drove the air inside out through the only avenue of escape—the opening at the base of the balloon. With a sizable fraction of its heated interior forcibly purged, the balloon and gondola were now no longer lighter than the surrounding air. The balloon began to plummet. Since it was only about fifty feet above the ground, and the envelope was still partially inflated, Bones figured Maddock had a decent chance of surviving the five-story drop mostly intact.

"Holy crap," Bones muttered. "He actually did it."

That was when the falling balloon erupted in flames.

Maddock saw none of this. Wholly engulfed by the collapsing balloon, he couldn't see anything but red. The impermeable fabric was covering his face, suffocating him. The heat was intense. Sauna hot… Pizza oven hot. He tried to wriggle out of his nylon shroud, but he couldn't even tell up from down.

This might not have been such a good idea, he thought, belatedly.

But he knew that, no matter what the outcome for him, he had succeeded. Fayed's balloon wouldn't be able to stay aloft. It would crash, and even if its deadly cargo was released, the exposure would be localized and minimal. Whatever happened to him, it had been worth it.

The impact with the ground was sudden and forceful, and yet not nearly as bad as he had expected. There was still enough air trapped in the folds of the balloon to cushion his landing, if only for a fraction of a second. Just enough to turn what had to have been a fifty-foot free fall into something that felt more like falling off the stage at a concert. It hurt, a lot, and he knew that if he somehow managed to extricate himself from the balloon, it would hurt a lot more in days to come, but everything still seemed to be connected and functional. The wind had been knocked out of him, but since he couldn't breathe anyway, he barely even noticed.

He fought to roll over, clawing at the fabric, trying to tear it away or at the very least, create some space to maneuver. Somehow, he managed to get his knees under him, and that gave him the leverage he needed to rip through a seam. He felt air on his face, hot and arid like the desert, but fresh, and he gasped in a lungful....

No, not so fresh after all. There was an odd smell wafting over him. A chemical odor, like a plastic bag full of celery set on fire.

Fire!

He struggled to get through the tear, widening it until head and shoulders were free, and twisted around until he spotted white smoke billowing up from the tangle of red fabric.

He had a pretty good idea what had happened. As soon as the balloon had begun losing altitude, the pilot—Fayed or one of his accomplices—had instinctively triggered the burners, sending a jet of flame high up into the balloon, but because the envelope had been deformed by Maddock's collision, the flames had come into direct contact with the highly flammable synthetic material, and subsequently, had been fanned into a raging conflagration as it fell to earth. Now, that blaze was sweeping across the billowing puddle of the settling balloon in which Maddock was still entangled.

He renewed his attack, tearing frantically at the ripped seam, an insect, struggling to get free of its cocoon. He got head and shoulders through, and then fought to get his feet under him, despite still being mostly covered by the balloon. The effort widened the tear, but in the process, he tripped, and stumbled forward, face-planting on the nylon-covered ground.

The smell was stronger now, almost overwhelming,

the fumes burned the back of his throat, and he could feel the heat rising at his back. He tried standing up on the move, half-running, half-crawling, but the balloon was caught on his feet, and even though he was moving, he was dragging it—and the flames—along with him.

He dropped flat again, intentionally this time, and rolled over onto his back, kicking at the fabric until, finally, the last remnants fell away and he was free. He backpedaled away, the flames now so close that he didn't dare take the time to turn around.

And then he felt the grit of the desert under his hands. He was clear of the balloon, clear of the approaching flames. He scurried back a few more feet and then collapsed backward, exhausted and aching, but mostly just relieved.

He had done it. He had stopped Fayed, and— impossibly— had lived to savor the victory.

Fayed!

Maddock felt a sudden tingle of apprehension. He rolled over and started to rise, but even as he did, he felt the other man's eyes on him. Nassir Fayed, looking every bit as bruised and battered as Maddock felt, stood just ten yards away, his face twisted with pain and rage. "I should have just killed you and left you in that tomb" he rasped.

Maddock didn't have the energy to form a witty riposte, so instead he just said, "Yeah. Big mistake." He sighed. "It's over, Fayed. You're finished."

Fayed's dust-streaked face was split with a fierce grimace. "Oh, no. It's not over. I still have the treasures. And I won't repeat the mistake of letting you live to interfere with my plans again."

The threat felt like more than just empty posturing.

Maddock's gaze flicked away from Fayed's face, just for a second. The other man was unarmed and appeared to be alone—if there had been another man with him in the balloon, he was either dead or unconscious somewhere beyond the burning wreckage—but over his shoulder, Maddock could see an approaching vehicle trailing a plume of dust as it crossed the open desert terrain, headed straight for them. It was the white van that had borne them away from Deir el-Medina; Fayed's van. Maddock surmised it had probably been lingering near the balloon staging area, the intended chase and recovery vehicle for the balloons.

He brought his eyes back to Fayed. "It won't matter. I'm not the only one who knows what you did. Bones and Nora will make sure the truth gets out."

"They won't live long enough to tell anyone. They won't be able to stay up there forever. When they come down, I'll be there to greet them. He nodded to a point over Maddock's shoulder. "Or maybe I won't have to wait."

Maddock turned and shot a glance in the direction Fayed had indicated. Behind him, not quite a hundred yards away, the second balloon was coming down. He could see Bones, a towering figure at the center of the gondola, working the vent and burner controls to simultaneously release hot air out the top, while replenishing it with quick bursts from the burner. The basket was just ten feet above the ground, dipping up and down a little, but maintaining a hover. Nora was leaning over the side, one hand cupped to her mouth as if shouting.

She *was* shouting, though Maddock could barely make out her words.

"Need a lift?"

Maddock brought his attention back to Fayed, just long enough to see that the van had almost reached them, then he turned and started running for the balloon.

A fresh surge of adrenaline numbed him to the pain of his bruises and infused him with a burst of energy. He could hear Fayed calling out to his accomplices, ordering them to run Maddock down, could hear the van's tires crunching across the desert floor behind him, getting louder with each passing second. He didn't look back, but when he sensed the van was nearly upon him, he veered to the right. A screech of brakes joined the tumult as the driver halted the vehicle and tried to change directions. Maddock continued zigzagging randomly as he closed the distance with the waiting balloon.

Ahead, Bones pulled the vent cord again, releasing another invisible plume of hot air from the top of the balloon, causing the gondola to drop down hard, and then bounce back into the air a foot or two. Nora was still shouting, and now he had no difficulty hearing her

"Hurry!"

He poured on a burst of speed, crossing the last few yards and leapt for the gondola, twisting over in mid-air like an Olympic high-jumper clearing the bar. Maddock's landing was nothing to be proud of, but the free-floating gondola absorbed some of the energy. Even as he tried to right himself, Bones, looming over him, pulled the burner handle for a long, sustained blast. With a full-throated roar, a pillar of fire rose into the cavernous envelope overhead.

Suddenly, the gondola jolted violently. With a great splintering sound, an entire section of the wicker basket caved in even as it swung away from the impact like a pendulum, spinning in circles beneath the balloon canopy. Bones kept the burner going, and as the gondola spun completely around, Maddock peered through the broken section of wicker weave and saw the roof of the white van that had just struck them, now falling away as they rose once more into the sky, out of reach.

Bones ran the burner for nearly a minute, rising so fast that the pressure in Maddock's ears became almost unbearable. For a few seconds, they were caught in the same breeze that had pushed them southeast after the initial takeoff, but as they rose even higher, a swift south wind caught them.

"Whoa," Bones exclaimed, letting go of the burner handle. "I think that's high enough for now."

Maddock edged closer to the hole in the side of the gondola and looked down. Although he had no way to accurately gauge their altitude, he guessed they were at least a thousand feet above the ground with the fertile green margin of the Nile disappearing behind them, and nothing but brown desert to their front. Because they were moving the same speed as the wind, the air felt still, but Maddock knew they were probably cruising along at a steady twenty-five miles per hour, maybe even faster than that.

"I guess we should put down soon," Bones said.

Maddock shook his head. "Not yet. Fayed is just waiting for us to set down. He can outrun us on the ground, follow us around and show up wherever we land."

"Well, if we don't set down soon, we'll wind up in the middle of BFE."

Nora gave him a perplexed frown. "BFE?"

"Ignore him," Maddock said, quickly. "We're heading pretty much north, right? Is there any kind of civilization in that direction?"

"Cairo," Nora replied, still frowning. "But I doubt we'll make it that far." She pointed behind them, indicating the river. "The Nile flows northeast past Luxor, but then turns west at Qena for more than fifty miles. If the wind does not change—and we do not run out of fuel—we will eventually cross it."

"And are there any towns out there?"

"There are settlements and farms all along the Nile Valley." Her face creased in though, and then she added. "If we can reach Qena, we can go to the Dendera Complex. Dr. Zahi should be there with Max Riddle."

"Dendera," Bones echoed. "Where they have the picture of the light bulb?"

"It's not a—"

"How far away is that?" Maddock cut in.

"It's about seventy kilometers along the river course to Qena, but if we continue in a straight line…" She shrugged. "Fifty kilometers?"

"Thirty miles," Maddock said. He glanced up at the balloon, wondering how much fuel it would take to keep the balloon aloft that long. If they were forced to land in the desert, they would have to walk the rest of the way, but at least that would put them out of Fayed's reach. "I say we go for it."

THIRTEEN

The wind bore them north, along the flanks of the sandstone cliffs of the Theban Hills. Bones and Maddock took turns at the burner control, sending up a jet of flame every few minutes to ensure that they maintained elevation and stayed in the wind. Although the air currents did not bring them any closer to the Nile, they never lost sight of the green ribbon that cut through the mostly featureless golden desert. After about forty-five minutes of this however, the river course made the left turn Nora had promised, cutting directly across their path.

Five minutes or so after that, the burner's flame began to sputter, barely reaching the opening to the balloon. Bones gave a heavy sigh. "Well, we knew that was gonna happen. What now?"

"I can see the highway below," Nora said. "If we can set down close to it, we should be able to find someone to give us a ride on to Dendera."

"Fayed might be down there, too," Bones pointed out.

Maddock shook his head. "One thing at a time. Right now, we need to focus on landing this thing, as opposed to crashing. One hot air balloon crash a day is my limit. Let's keep whatever fuel we have left for braking, and see where we end up."

Without frequent blasts from the burner to keep the air hot, the balloon soon began to lose altitude. The rate of their descent was considerably slower than that of a skydiver under a parachute, but Maddock knew that when the air cooled to the same temperature as the surrounding sky, they would simply plummet. He curled his hand around the burner control, and waited for that inevitable moment to arrive. With a little luck, there would be enough fuel left to moderate their descent all the way to the ground. If not….

He didn't want to think about that.

The wind carried them another mile or two closer to the elbow-bend in the river, almost to the green margin of the valley, but then they dropped out of the current that had borne them north, and descended into a gentler breeze that carried them west, back out toward the open desert. Maddock debated giving the burners a quick blast to get back up into the faster winds aloft, but decided that reaching solid ground was the more immediate priority. As they got closer to the ground however, entering an area of relatively high air pressure, the rate of descent slowed almost to nothing, while the wind from the east continued pushing them further from the river valley.

Maddock decided to risk venting some of the hot air, and was immediately rewarded with a feeling of lightness. He released the pull handle, but the feeling did not go away. "Going down!"

Bones, watching their descent from the edge of the gondola, nodded but was silent for several seconds. Then, he shouted. "Better put on the brakes!"

Maddock pulled the burner control on the first word, holding the sputtering flame for a full five seconds.

"Still falling."

He pulled again, the flame no longer a continuous tongue of bright orange, but rather an eruption of short, sooty yellow spurts, and held it until Bones finally waved his hand to indicate that they were rising again. A look through the broken side of the gondola revealed the ground, now only about twenty feet below them, and rolling past with unnerving swiftness. Although they couldn't feel it, they were caught in what had to be at least a ten-mile-an-hour breeze.

Ten miles an hour didn't seem very fast, but trying to land a lighter-than-air aircraft, which had no means of anchoring in place, much less putting on the brakes, was going to be a tricky proposition. "We're going to have to bail out," he announced, and then directing his words at Nora, added, "I'll hit the vent and try to get us a little closer. As soon as we bump, you jump. But don't try to stay on your feet. Tuck and roll."

She nodded, soberly.

"What about that stuff?" Bones said, jerking a thumb at the garbage bags full of mold spores.

"We should destroy them," Nora said, immediately.

Maddock shook his head. "Let's hang onto them Right now, they're the only proof we have of what Fayed planned."

Bones grinned as if he knew a secret, but then scooped both bags up and promptly pitched them out of the gondola. Then, he helped Nora climb onto the padded edge in preparation for her jump.

Maddock pulled the vent release, and a moment later, the basket crunched against the desert floor. Nora cried out and then was gone. The gondola bounced back into the air for a second or two but then came down again and began scraping across the ground.

Bones, shouting, "Hoooo leeeee craaaap!" hurled himself out. Close on his heels, and feeling a sense of déjà vu, Maddock leapt from the gondola for the second time that day.

Heeding his own advice, he bent his knees to absorb

the energy of landing and threw himself to the side, rolling on the hard ground until the last of his forward momentum was exhausted. When he raised his head, he saw that the balloon, now empty of passengers, had risen a few feet off the ground and, still caught in the ten-mile-an-hour breeze, was sailing away across the desert like a ghost ship.

He rose gingerly, wincing at yet another set of bruises and scrapes, and turned to look for the others. Bones had already regained his feet and was helping Nora to stand, about a hundred feet further back. Both were gazing across the desert toward the dark smudge that was the Nile Valley.

"Guess we've got some walking to do," he said as he joined them.

"Maybe not," Bones countered, pointing toward the horizon.

Maddock followed his line of sight and spotted a plume of dust rising above the desert floor. A vehicle was approaching.

Even from a distance, Maddock could see that it was not Fayed's white van, but he remained wary as the vehicle—a battered old truck that looked like a cast-off military deuce-and-a-half—rolled up beside them. A wizened old Egyptian in a rumpled jellabiya got out and started speaking in rapid-fire Arabic.

Nora answered in the same language, which seemed to puzzle the old man, but only for a moment. The back and forth continued for a little while, then Nora turned and provided a quick summary of the exchange. "He's from a nearby farm. He saw the balloon coming down and decided to investigate. He'll take us to Dendera, but he'll want compensation."

"Tell him to bill Fayed for it," Bones suggested.

Nora grinned and then passed this along to the old farmer. After a moment's consideration, he shrugged and returned to the cab of his truck. When he was seated, he made a "come on" gesture and barked a quick command which needed no translation.

After retrieving the bags of mold toxin, they settled in for a short ride to the Dendera ruins, which were perched on the edge of the desert, only about five miles from where they had come down.

The Dendera Complex was not as well-organized or majestic as the Temple of Hatshepsut, but it seemed more authentic to Maddock. Perhaps that was due to the fact that, unlike the complex at Deir el-Bahari, there were no tour buses, no crowds of visitors smelling of sun screen. The site wasn't deserted, but it was definitely a lot quieter. But more than that, the Dendera ruins felt like actual ruins, with broken columns and crumbling walls. The entrance to the temple complex was an enormous free-standing doorway, the stone lintel easily fifty feet above the ground, but to either side, where there ought to have been walls to support it, there were only a few jumbled stone blocks. A headless statue of a reclining lion guarded the left side of the approach—the weathered lump of stone on the platform on the opposite side was all that remained of its twin—and directly behind it was a twelve-foot high stone block engraved with the likenesses of Egyptian gods.

"This is the Gate of Domitian and Trajan," Nora said, unable to completely set aside her professorial inclination to lecture. "Or what's left of it."

Maddock recognized the names. "Roman emperors?"

"Most of the structures here date back only as far as the Ptolemaic dynasty, with most of the recent additions dating to the Roman period, though this has been an important religious center for at least four thousand years."

They moved through the gate and down a paved walk that bisected a large courtyard littered with the stumps of broken pillars, toward an enormous stone building that appeared to be mostly intact.

"The Temple of Hathor," Nora said. "Even though it was built by Greco-Roman rulers in the First Century C.E. the temple utilizes the most ancient and sacred style of Egyptian architecture—the mastaba. That word is Arabic—it means 'stone bench'—but the Egyptian word *pr-djed,* translates as 'House of Eternity.' The oldest tombs in Egypt, pre-dating even the Old Kingdom, were mastabas. The first pyramid ever built, the Step Pyramid of Djoser at Saqqara, is simply a stack of six mastabas, each one smaller than the one under it."

The Temple of Hathor was not solid like a pyramid however. Halfway up its steeply sloping sides, the front wall opened up to reveal six massive pillars supporting the roof. Each of the pillars was topped with what appeared to be a female head with thick bundles of hair falling down to either side, but the faces had been erased by weather, or more likely, vandalism. Beyond the entrance, the dimly lit interior featured still more pillars and columns, all of them engraved with hieroglyphics and larger figures from the Egyptian pantheon, many of them trimmed with sky blue paint.

Nora led them through the large enclosure, which she identified as "the Large Hypostyle Hall," and through a maze of passages to a set of stairs descending into the crypts beneath the Temple. Every square inch of stone bore some kind of carving or inscription, even the ceilings, and while some had suffered the ravages of time, other images were startlingly distinct. As they moved along, Maddock heard voices coming from further up the passage—two men engaged in conversation about the Temple and its decorations. He knew this because they were speaking English. He also recognized both voices.

"But you have to admit," Max Riddle was saying, "It does look like a light bulb."

"Does it?" countered Zahi Mohamed. "Have you ever seen a lightbulb with a snake inside? A light bulb coming out of a lotus flower?"

As Maddock and the others rounded a corner, they could see a small cluster of people in the passage ahead, bathed in the glow of artificial light from handheld umbrella lights.

"Well, no, but those could be symbolic," said Riddle.

"Symbolic," Zahi said, his tone victorious. "Exactly. But symbolizing what? The lotus flower and the serpent are found everywhere in the art of Ancient Egypt. They symbolize the fertility of the Nile—a symbol of enduring life for all of Egypt."

Nora glanced back at Bones. "Told you."

Their arrival once again attracted the attention of the production crew, but this time, Zahi didn't wait for the "cut" command. When his gaze fell upon Nora, he scowled and pushed through the videographers to confront them. The lights and cameras followed him, as did Riddle.

"What are you doing here?" he demanded. "I already gave you permission to conduct your survey."

Nora hastened to meet him. "Dr. Zahi, I have so much to tell you. We found the tomb of Smenkhkare and Neferneferuaten."

Zahi folded his arms and scowled. "That is ridiculous. No such tombs exist."

"I can take you there," she insisted. "There is an entrance at Deir el-Medina. But first, I must tell you about Fayed—"

Maddock heard shouts from behind them. He turned, and saw a small knot of men hastening toward them. Most wore khaki uniforms with badges and dark berets, and had their pistols drawn and aimed at Maddock and the others. The only unarmed member of the group wore street clothes that were torn, and streaked with dust and sweat.

Nassir Fayed.

"Speak of the devil," Maddock muttered.

FOURTEEN

Eyes blazing with righteous indignation, Fayed stalked toward them. "I knew I would find you here," he snarled, then looked past them to Zahi. "I don't know what lies they have told you, but these people are looters and terrorists. This woman lied to me about what she had discovered, and has been working with these men to steal the treasures for sale on the black market."

"Dude, you know we just got here this morning," Bones protested.

"And left a trail of destruction across half of Luxor," Fayed shot back. "When I discovered their treachery, they tried to kill me, and were preparing to release a biological agent to hide their crimes.

"He lies," Nora cried out. "He is the one who stole the treasures from the tomb. He was going to release these—" She pointed to the bags Maddock and Bones were still holding. "A toxin made from the mold found in the tomb."

"Silence," Fayed barked. "You will see how we deal with foreigners and women," by his tone it was difficult to guess which he despised more, "who try to destroy our heritage." He turned to the closest policeman, who wore three stars on his epaulets, and barked a command in Arabic. The man repeated the command to his men, and they all swarmed forward.

Maddock quickly raised the plastic bag over his head, curling his fingers into the pliable surface. "You don't want to do that," he warned.

The policemen halted their advance, evidently understanding the threat, but did not lower their weapons.

"Shoot them!" screamed Fayed.

The police officers did not comply, but Maddock knew the standoff couldn't last. They would have to surrender or be killed, and since he doubted they would be given anything remotely resembling due process in the Egyptian court system, their only hope was to convince Zahi that they were telling the truth.

Without lowering the bag, he turned to Zahi. Behind the archaeologist, Max Riddle and his crew had retreated a few steps, and were ducking low in anticipation of a hailstorm of bullets, but their cameras were still running, capturing everything.

"Look," he said, striving for a calming tone. "We really did just get here this morning. We were surveying the well, just like we said we would, when someone bombed the entrance and tried to kill us. We swam out through the underwater passage and found the tomb. The treasure chamber had already been cleaned out. Do you really think we could have accomplished all that in a couple hours? We can take you to the tomb. You can see for yourself."

Zahi stared back, his face a mask of uncertainty. "I would very much like to see this tomb. But you would have me believe that Fayed is responsible for these crimes? You would ask me to take your word over his?" He shook his head. "No, there will have to be an investigation, and until that time... I'm sorry, but you must be taken into custody, or face immediate consequences."

"Don't take our word for it. We can prove it," Bones said. "I can show you right now."

"Ridiculous," Fayed snapped. "They are stalling. Shoot them."

"Seriously, dude. You probably don't want to do that. You know what's in these bags. The Pharaoh's Curse. Is that how you want to die? I can prove we're telling the truth. I grabbed Uma's SD card before Fayed's goons dragged us out of the tomb. I've got video of the whole thing."

For the first time since making his tempestuous arrival, Fayed looked nervous. "Video? That's hardly proof of anything. You fabricated it."

"See for yourself." Bones turned and looked past Zahi to the *Maximum Mysteries* production team. "Max, you can do playback on your cameras, right?"

Riddle stood, a little hesitantly, and then, realizing that this was a chance at taking the spotlight, stepped forward briskly. "Absolutely." He then faced one of his videographers, but instead of asking the man for his camera, he started speaking. "Folks, this is an incredible development. Not only are we about to see footage from an undiscovered Egyptian tomb, but we're also going to solve a real-life mystery." He paused a beat, and then in a slightly less solemn tone, continued. "That was good right? Yeah?"

Maddock glanced over at Bones, who just rolled his eyes.

Riddle turned to another of his crew. "Josh, let's put this on the Max-Cam,"

"This is completely inappropriate," Fayed cried. "If this video footage exists, it should be seized as evidence."

Zahi raised a hand to silence him, and in a calm voice, said, "I would like to see it." The archaeologist then turned to the police officer and, still speaking English, added, "Captain, I think it would be best if you and your men put your guns away. Post a guard. No one should be allowed to leave." His gaze flicked meaningfully toward Fayed.

Fayed whirled and tried to flee, but the way was blocked by the squad of policemen who, without needing to be told, had grasped the changing nature of the situation. One of them grabbed the hotelier by the arm and spun him around, propelling him forward again. The police captain gave Fayed a hard look, and then nodded to Zahi. "I too would like to see this evidence."

Zahi turned to Maddock. "Does that satisfy you?"

"It's a start," Maddock answered, and then lowered the bag of mold toxins, placing it on the stone floor.

Bones did likewise, and then took the postage stamp-sized SD card from his pocket. As he handed it to a waiting Max Riddle, he glanced at the relief carving on the wall beside him and did a double-take. "Huh," he said, and then glanced back at Nora. "Sure looks like a light bulb to me."

FIFTEEN

They arrived back in Deir el-Medina just as the sun was dipping behind the Theban Hills. Amun Ra, his crossing of the sky now complete, was about to begin his nightly passage through the Underworld, but this time, he would have some company, at least for the first few hundred feet of the journey.

Dr. Zahi, eager to see the newly discovered tomb for himself, had insisted on going directly there from Dendera, and in a move that came as a surprise to no one who knew him, had agreed to allow Max Riddle to accompany him inside to record the moment for posterity.

Maddock suspected that Riddle would have preferred to have Nora leading the tour of the tomb, for reasons other than her obvious expertise as the actual discoverer, but knew well enough not to challenge Zahi's authority. Nora, too, seemed to understand that this would be Zahi's show, and hung back with Maddock and Bones as the production crew moved into the descending passage that led down to the tomb's rear entrance.

"Do you think they'll be able to track down all the treasure Fayed stole?" Maddock asked Nora, as they waited their turn.

"If I know Zahi, he will pressure the prosecutors to offer leniency in exchange for cooperation."

The video footage from Uma's camera had been sufficiently damning to warrant Fayed's immediate arrest. Maddock guessed they would be asked to testify against the man at some future date, and he wasn't looking forward to having to explain some of the things they had done trying to stop Fayed's mad scheme but, for the moment at least, no one seemed interested in holding them accountable.

"Well that's a bunch of crap," Bones said. "That assclown wasn't just a tomb robber. He was planning mass murder."

"Recovering the cultural treasure of Egypt is far more important than taking the proverbial pound of flesh." She gave a weary sigh. "Of course, even if we get it all back, the damage has been done. The site is no longer pristine. We've missed our chance to examine the artifacts *in situ*."

"Well aren't you just a ray of sunshine," Maddock retorted with a chuckle.

Nora managed a wan smile. "You're right of course. This is an amazing discovery. And it's all thanks to you two." She gave him a sidelong glance. I guess you finished the job you came here to do. What's next for you?"

"Finished?" Maddock replied. "By my reckoning, we explored less than a third of the passage. Who's to say that's the only tomb down there."

Nora clearly had not considered this, and an eager gleam appeared in her eyes. "It's possible," she said, nodding. "And you would do that? Stay and continued the survey?"

"I hate leaving a job half-done. Or rather one-third done. Besides, we have to go back in to recover Uma's computer. I hope Fayed didn't send anyone back to get rid of Uma and the rest of our gear."

Bones let out a menacing growl, "If that bastard did something to Uma, he won't live long enough to beg for leniency."

Uma wasn't exactly where Bones had left her, but she

was close. One of the production assistants had relocated the little submersible to the passage just outside the empty canopic chamber. Bones knelt and performed a quick start-up inspection.

The crew had moved on to the burial chamber. Maddock could hear Zahi expostulating about the history of the two little-known historical figures who had ruled Egypt in the brief interval between Akhenaten and Tutankhamun.

"Everything looks okay," Bones reported. "We'll need to get a new SD card and charge the batteries, but I think she's good to go."

"Then the rest of our stuff is probably still there at the entrance," said Maddock. "We'll have to get our tanks refilled, and maybe rent a compressor and a scooter. First thing tomorrow, we'll have to drive to the coast and find a dive shop."

"I can take you," Nora said, then after a moment's consideration, added, "I hope Fayed didn't do anything to my car."

"If he did, we'll just steal one of his," Bones promised, and then laughed at Nora's horrified expression. "That takes care of tomorrow, but what are we gonna do until then?"

"I was thinking sleep might be nice," Maddock said.

"Sleep? Dude, there's plenty of time to sleep when we're dead." He turned to Nora. "So what is there to do in this town?"

Nora opened her mouth to answer, but then closed it again and frowned. "I think we've already done it all."

"Well, crap," Bones said, laughing. "You know, we wouldn't be having this problem if we'd gone to the other Luxor."

Maddock just shook his head.

The End

If you enjoyed *Destination-Luxor*, try *Outpost,* book one of the *Elementals* trilogy!

Enjoy this preview of

OUTPOST
A Dane Maddock Adventure

"We got a hit!"

Dane Maddock looked away from the view through the forward windscreen—a vast, limitless expanse of deep sapphire blue water, dazzling in the afternoon sun—and over to the console where his friend Corey Dean sat hunched over the display of a laptop computer. Before Maddock could ask Corey to elaborate, the imposing six-and-a-half-foot tall form of Maddock's partner and soon-to-be brother-in-law, Uriah "Bones" Bonebrake, appeared in the doorway behind him.

"Did we find it?" Bones asked, eagerly.

"Not sure what we found," Corey said, peering at the screen. "It's big."

"That's what she said," Bones quipped.

Corey studied the image a few seconds longer, then leaned back with a disappointed sigh. "But it's not big enough."

"That's what she said to Maddock," Bones said.

Maddock, who had long ago developed an immunity to his friend's off-color put downs, heard the note of disappointment in Bones' voice. "What are we looking at, Corey?"

Corey turned the screen so Maddock could see it from the helm station. The image was orange and grainy, a computer-generated visual interpretation of sound waves bouncing off the sea floor. To an untrained eye, it looked like so much static, but Maddock had seen enough side-scan sonar profiles to recognize the straight lines of a manmade object. Corey however was the expert.

"It's in several pieces. Whatever it was broke up before it reached the bottom. This largest piece is what got my attention. It's long and narrow—"

Maddock leveled a finger at Bones. "Don't say it."

Bones just kept grinning.

"I'd say about a hundred feet in length," Corey said. "The Waratah was five hundred feet long. There's not enough debris to indicate a ship that large."

Maddock stared at the image intently. "Judging by the shape, I'd be more inclined to say we're looking at an aircraft. Anything like that on the charts?"

"Let me check." Corey tapped in a few commands, then managed a hopeful grin. "Nope. We're the first to record anything here."

'Here' was the waters of the continental shelf about two hundred miles off the tip of South Africa. Maddock and his treasure-hunting crew—Bones and Corey, along with Willis Sanders and Matt Barnaby—were plying the waters of the southern hemisphere aboard his 80-foot motor yacht Sea Foam, halfway around the world from their usual stomping grounds in the Atlantic, to investigate the almost legendary disappearance of the S.S. Waratah.

In 1909, the Waratah, a five-hundred foot long cargo-liner with 211 passengers and crew aboard, had left Durban for Cape Town, on its way to London, and promptly vanished. Subsequent searches for the missing ship had only deepened the mystery.

Early on, it was believed that the Waratah was still afloat, abandoned and adrift, but extremely high seas prevented Royal Navy search vessels from entering the area where the ship was thought to be. Ten days later, the Australian government received a cable notifying them that a ship believed to be the Waratah had been spotted, steaming toward Durban, but that ship, whatever it was, never reached port. Three days after that, two different ships reported seeing bodies in the water near the mouth of a river two hundred miles southwest of Durban, but none were positively identified as passengers from the missing vessel. In 1912, a life-preserver with the name of the ship washed up in New Zealand, and thirteen years after that, a pilot flying over the same section of coast reported a wreck that he believed was the Waratah. Subsequent attempts to locate the wreck had failed to produce anything remotely definitive, but despite, or perhaps because of those failures, the quest to find the Waratah had taken on an almost mythic proportions. Some had taken to calling it Australia's Titanic.

Maddock thought it was a fool's errand, but a wealthy action-adventure novelist with a passion for finding lost shipwrecks had come to him with a lucrative contract to conduct yet another search for the legendary vessel, this time in open water rather than along the coast where all previous expeditions had focused their attention. It was an offer Maddock couldn't reasonably refuse. Even if the search yielded no results, which was the most probable outcome, it was a valuable connection that might lead to other, more rewarding expeditions.

Now it seemed, the deal had produced some unexpected, if unrelated fruit.

"Finding the Waratah was always a long shot, but maybe we can solve another maritime mystery that slipped through the cracks." He pulled the throttle controls back, reversing the screws. "Might as well get some pictures before we go."

Bones grinned. "I'll get Uma prepped."

Uma was Bones' nickname for their ROV—remotely operated underwater vehicle. Although Maddock and Bones, along with their fellow crewman Willis Sanders, were all former Navy SEALs and experienced divers, there were limits to what they could accomplish with SCUBA equipment. Uma could go places that they simply could not. Places like the ocean floor nearly half-a-mile beneath Sea Foam's hull.

By the time Maddock had the boat positioned above the location Corey had identified, Bones was ready to put Uma in the water. The little submersible was equipped with a high-resolution digital video camera and a powerful searchlight, but there was very little to see during the descent. The screen displaying Uma's video feed remained an unchanging black, so Maddock kept his eye on the horizon. The seas were thankfully calm, but the area they were in, at the boundary between the Indian and Atlantic Oceans, was known for rogue waves, one of which had probably been responsible for sinking the Waratah. Conditions under the water would be even more challenging since the collision of oceans created extraordinarily strong submerged currents. Bones was uncharacteristically subdued, focused intently on piloting Uma into the depths.

It took about fifteen minutes for the little submersible to reach the bottom and another five to locate the wreck. Maddock now turned his attention to the video screen, watching intently as Uma's searchlight and camera revealed the submerged landscape. The sea floor was uniformly flat and everything was a dull beige, the color of sediment. Then, with almost no warning, the wreck appeared.

"As usual, Maddock," Bones announced. "You were half-right,"

Maddock saw immediately what his friend meant. Although lightly dusted by an accretion of sediment, there was no mistaking what they were looking at: not one, but two airplane fuselages, though it was hard to tell where one ended and the other began. The aircraft were entangled like conjoined twins.

Corey shook his head in disbelief. "How did that happen?"

"Probably a mid-air collision," Maddock said. "Looks like the smaller plane almost took the tail off the bigger one."

Bones moved Uma in closer, revealing broken struts and the stubs where the wings had been sheared off. The smaller plane was about one-third the size of the other, and appeared to have been a biplane with an open cockpit. The larger aircraft actually did look more like a ship at first glance, with a wide-body that seemed better suited to riding on the high seas than cruising at high altitude, but part of one wing remained attached, complete with a single engine nacelle, sprouting three twisted propeller blades.

"Talk about a blast from the past," Corey said. "Those are vintage. How old do you think they are?"

Maddock shook his head. "Hard to say. Bones, try blowing some of that silt away. See if you can find any identifying marks."

Bones brought the ROV in even closer, until it was practically sitting in the crumpled cockpit of the smaller biplane, then turned it around and hit the thrusters, sending out a blast of water that stirred up the sediment. Uma shot away, but Bones quickly brought her back around and shone the spotlight into the cloud rising above the wreck. It only took a few minutes for the current to sweep away the sediment, revealing the instrument panel and old-fashioned stick controls. There were actually two seats in the cockpit, but both were empty. Either the crew had bailed out before the crash, or their bones had long since dissolved away.

Seeing nothing distinctive enough to make an identification of the aircraft, Bones pulled Uma back and then cautiously piloted her through the gaping hole in the top of the larger plane's fuselage.

Maddock felt a chill as the bulkheads comprising the plane's interior seemed to close around him. Unlike the cockpit of the smaller biplane, this felt much more like a place where men had died, sealed into a coffin for burial at sea. The interior reminded him a little of the cargo bay of a modern military transport plane, which perhaps contributed to his sense of foreboding. He wasn't claustrophobic, but he felt strangely anxious, and had to resist the urge to tell Bones to back away.

Uma moved down the length of the cargo bay, the camera scanning every shadowy corner for anything that might help identify the aircraft but as with the smaller plane, there were no distinguishing features.

"Might as well wrap it up," Maddock said. "We can get some more exterior shots and send them to Jimmy. Maybe he can do some computer magic and get us a positive ID."

If anyone could identify the wrecked airplanes from photographs, it was Maddock's old pal Jimmy Letson. Jimmy was both an ace investigative reporter and a computer whiz, and frequently helped Maddock out with research into subjects ranging from ancient shipwrecks to diabolical global conspiracies.

"Wait a sec," Bones said, backing Uma up and tilting her down a few degrees. "Look at that."

The image on the screen showed a misshapen triangle, made of what appeared to be black metal, lying on the deck, partly buried in silt.

"What is that?" Corey said. "A piece of the propeller?"

"It looks more like an axe head," Maddock said. "The wooden handle probably rotted away."

"Close." Bones brought the ROV in even closer until the object almost filled up the screen. "It's a tomahawk."

Maddock glanced over at his friend, skeptically. "You're sure?"

"Trust me on this, kemosabe."

Maddock almost regretted having raised the question. Bones, a Cherokee Indian, was not likely to make a mistake about that.

Bones traced the outline of the object on the screen. "You can tell by the curve of the blade, and this spike on the back end. They don't really make 'em like that anymore."

"What I mean is, what's a tomahawk doing on an old airplane off the coast of South Africa?"

"Looks like there's an engraving on it," Corey said, peering at the close-up. "Can't make out what it says. A name maybe? And that looks like a date on the bottom. Nineteen-fifty-eight. Wow. You're right, Bones. That is old."

Maddock stared at screen for a minute. "That's not a nine. It's a seven. Seventeen-fifty-eight."

Corey looked again, wide-eyed. "Holy crap."

Maddock nodded. "I think we should bring it up."

ABOUT THE AUTHORS

David Wood is the USA Today bestselling author of the action-adventure series, The Dane Maddock Adventures, and many other works. He also writes fantasy under his David Debord pen name. When not writing, he hosts the Wood on Words podcast. David and his family live in Santa Fe, New Mexico. Visit him online at davidwoodweb.com.

Sean Ellis has authored and co-authored more than two dozen action-adventure novels, including the Nick Kismet adventures, the Jack Sigler/Chess Team series with Jeremy Robinson, and the Jade Ihara adventures with David Wood. He served with the Army National Guard in Afghanistan, and has a Bachelor of Science degree in Natural Resources Policy from Oregon State University. Sean is also a member of the International Thriller Writers organization. He currently resides in Arizona, where he divides his time between writing, adventure sports, and trying to figure out how to save the world. Learn more at seanellisauthor.com.